I0744680

Daddy Doctor To The Rescue

A DDLG and ABDL romantic love story about a baby girl who becomes her Daddy Dom's favorite patient

By Tina Moore

© Copyright 2019 by Tina Moore

All rights reserved.

The content contained within this book may not be reproduced, duplicated, or transmitted without direct written permission from the author or the publisher.

Under no circumstances will any blame or legal responsibility be held against the publisher, or author, for any damages, reparation, or monetary loss due to the information contained within this book, either directly or indirectly.

Legal Notice:

This book is copyright protected. It is only for personal use. You cannot amend, distribute, sell, use, quote or paraphrase any part, or the content within this book, without the consent of the author or publisher.

Table of Contents

Chapter 1

"Ms. Banks, you stand accused of possession of MDMA and public indecency. How do you plead?" The judge peered at me over the rim of his small, rectangular glasses. The look on his ancient face made it seem like he could see into my very soul, and he did not like what he saw there. What he saw was a scrawny, five-foot-nothing girl with unkempt black hair, a dirty black tank top, ripped black stockings and smeared mascara. It had been a rough night.

"Guilty, your Honor," I said, my voice cracking a bit. On the outside, I may have looked like a wild party girl, but the reality was that I was closer to a scared schoolgirl who had been sent to the principal's office. I didn't have much of a case, there was a video of the whole thing from the cop's body camera, and my lawyer thought I could get a better deal if I threw myself on the mercy of the court. The judge nodded, took off his glasses, and crossed his wrinkled hands, considering for a moment.

"Your court-appointed attorney filled me in on your history. Very sad to lose both of your parents so young. You grew up in foster care, and you've been in and out of jail ever since your foster parents threw you out last year. I don't see a permanent address listed here for you. Where are you staying currently?" Again, that soul-piercing gaze. I cleared my throat before speaking, hoping my voice wouldn't crack.

"With friends, your honor," I squeak.

"I see. Is there anything else you'd like to add or does that bring us more or less up to speed?" He questioned.

"It does your Honor," I reply. I know that I probably haven't made a very good impression, but I have no defense for my stupid actions. My "rap sheet" sounded more impressive than it actually was. Most of it was just dumb stunts done in an attempt to impress whatever boy had caught my eye that week. They never stuck around, though, no matter how impressive my stunts were.

"Well, I have some good news for you, although you may not see it as such at first. There is a rehab facility that specializes in troubled young women, such as yourself. Their technique is highly experimental, but it has yielded promising results. Rather than another fruitless stint in jail, I sentence you to thirty days of treatment at the Franken Institute for Young Women," he said.

Rehab?! I was astounded. I wasn't a junkie. I just liked to have a good time, get a little loose, and forget my troubles for a bit. I did not need rehab.

"But, sir -" I was cut off the judge's hammer signaling an end to the session. Everyone began to shuffle around, and my court-appointed attorney took off without so much as wishing me "good luck." There would be no appeal. The bailiff began escorting me back to holding. I sneered at him to cover up the fact that I just wanted to curl up into a ball and cry, hoping that I looked a lot tougher than I felt.

"A van will be along shortly to take you to the facility," the bailiff said before shoving me roughly back into my cell. I sat on my hard cot and waited, trying to keep up a tough facade in case any of the other inmates were in the mood to start something. Inside, however, my mind was spinning. I had not meant to get arrested. No one ever does, I suppose. I had only agreed to hold on to ecstasy to impress Tyler, yet another in a long string of boys who I would never hear from again. I never even got to take any before getting busted. As soon as the handcuffs came out, Tyler and his friends were nowhere to be seen, and I was left to fend for myself. Typical, stupid me.

I lied down on the miserably hard cot. The long night of drinking and dancing was beginning to catch up to me, and I longed for sleep, yet I couldn't get comfortable on the hard cot. Even if I could, the disastrous night would keep repeating in my head anyway. The way Tyler and his friends kept egging me on, daring me to do more and more ridiculous things until I found myself flashing a cop while Tyler laughed and recorded me with his phone. That laughter was still ringing in my ears, mocking me. I covered my eyes and rolled over onto my side, trying to find a more comfortable position but a loose spring poked me in the rib. Hopefully, this rehab place would have decent beds. That would be something to look forward to, at least.

Chapter 2

I finally got some rest during the drive to the rehab facility, the gentle swaying of the van rocking me to sleep. I woke with a start as a pair of massive, rusty gates protested loudly as they slowly swung open. I looked out of the van windows to see a few sad trees peppered around a mostly empty parking lot.

What a dump. I rolled my eyes and slumped down in my seat, sulking. I knew that I should be grateful that I wasn't in jail, but I couldn't bring myself to be happy about being involuntarily confined with a bunch of drug addicts. Who knows what kind of dangerous freaks waited for me inside?

As we pulled up to the nondescript brick building, two orderlies opened the van door and looked at me expectantly. I knew what they wanted of me, but I was feeling particularly bratty, so I just sat there, not moving.

"Ms. Banks, step out of the vehicle, please," one of them said in the deep, commanding voice of someone who is used to being listened to. I stuck my tongue out at him before turning my face to the window and crossing my arms over my chest. I may have been court-ordered to be here, but I didn't have to make it easy for them.

Strong hands wrapped around my arms and before I knew it, I was over his shoulder! I could feel my skirt blow up, and I knew that my panties were being exposed for everyone to see. I knew he was trying to humiliate me, but this was hardly the first time I'd been ass-up in front of a crowd of people. My instinct was to give this guy an earful to let him know who he was dealing, but I stopped myself. I knew from experience that you could push these guys, but only so far before they "accidentally" sucker-punched you in the eye. I decided on a softer approach.

"They should put a saddle on you," I said as casually as possible.

"Your human rickshaw service only gets two stars from me. I'm sorry to say. Bony shoulders, would not ride again," I angrily said.

"Shut up," he muttered and brought me inside. I grinned, feeling like I had gotten away with something. It may have been a stupid, small victory, but it was mine, and I was going to enjoy it. He came to a stop by the front desk and unceremoniously dumped me onto the floor. I landed badly on my ankle but didn't give him the satisfaction of letting on. Once upright, I saw that the place was a bit nicer on the inside. It had a cozy, if somewhat institutional, feel. There were oversized chairs and couches in the lobby and hotel art lining the walls. The carpet was a terrible lime green that looked so old. It probably should have been in a museum. I didn't mind it, however. It gave the place a bit more character.

Maybe this place won't be so bad after all. I dared to hope as I looked around.

A middle-aged woman in a sweater and khakis, who seemed to have been waiting for our arrival, saw us come in and approached us. She had a broad, matronly face and a name tag that said, "Deborah."

"Has this one been giving you trouble, Sam?" she said, assessing me with a cold, dispassionate gaze.

"Not too much, ma'am," he said. "Just some first day jitters, I imagine," he replied. He may not have been articulate, but at least he wasn't a snitch. She gave a curt nod.

"Very good. Show her to her room," she said. She addressed me directly, her voice cold and stiff.

"I'll be along shortly to give you your first treatment, young lady," she said. I tried not to show it outwardly, but the way she said that made me feel nervous. No one had yet bothered to explain to me what kind of treatments I would be getting at this rehab place. I just hoped it wouldn't be group therapy. Group therapy sessions always just turned in a trauma competition without fail. Sam took me gently by the elbow and showed me to a tiny little room with just enough space for a twin bed and a nightstand. As he closed the door behind him, I heard a lock slide into place. Here I was, locked up yet again. I sat on the tiny bed and tried not to cry.

I waited for what felt like hours, but I had no way of telling how much time had passed. Finally, Deborah unlocked the door and instructed me to follow her. She led me to a communal bathroom and told me to shower. I was grateful for the chance to get clean. It had been well over a day since I had last showered and I probably stank to high heaven. The water was hot and soothing, but when I tried to linger under the calming spray, Deborah barked at me to wrap it up. When I emerged from the shower stall wrapped in a towel, I saw that the clothes I had arrived in were gone. In their place was a neatly folded nightgown with an adult diaper sitting on top. I eyed it warily, unsure why they would think I would need that.

"I can go to the bathroom on my own, you know," I said, gesturing towards the diaper. Deborah only shook her head and tutted.

"Potties are for big girls. Babies wear diapers. Put on your diaper, little one. It's time to feed you and put you to bed," she said. I stared at her, speechless. I thought for a moment that she must be joking or might be having some fit, but she only matched my gaze with another icy stare.

"Are you going to be a good girl and do as Nanny says or shall I call Sam in to do it for you?" Deborah asked. The thought of that giant, ogre of a man putting a diaper on me was too embarrassing even to consider. Reluctantly, I complied and slid the diaper on, feeling like an absolute fool. The diaper made me feel puffy and bloated, and I was grateful that the oversized, shapeless nightgown hid that I was wearing it. I felt utterly ridiculous and was very glad that there was no one to see my shame.

Deborah led me back to my room. While I was showering, someone had brought in a tray with a baby bottle and a pacifier. Deborah sat on my bed and patted her lap, indicating that I should sit. I hesitated in the doorway, briefly wondering if I had gotten high somehow, like some flashback.

"This is weird. What's happening?" I asked, my eyes shifting nervously around the room. Deborah rolled her eyes and sighed. Her voice took on a lilting, patient tone as though she were speaking to a small child.

"You have been a very naughty girl, that is why the judge sent you to us. It's not your fault, of course, you didn't have a Nanny like me to raise you to be a good girl. Doctor Franken has designed a treatment for little girls like you so that we can get all those mean, nasty thoughts out of your head that are making you be naughty and help you to be the good girl that we know that you can be," she explained. She smiled at me expectantly as though that cleared everything up. I stared at her for a moment, still thoroughly confused. Then, I suddenly remembered an article I saw while waiting at the health clinic about age regression therapy. I didn't read it, of course, but it was full of hilarious pictures of grown adults in diapers, sucking on pacifiers. And now it was happening to me of all the rotten luck. I hesitated near the doorway and considered my options: throw a tantrum and end up being force-fed by Sam the orderly or play along until it was time to be released from this weird place. I decided the second choice seemed like the easiest, at least for now, and sat uneasily on Deborah's lap.

How bad could it be, after all? I thought to myself. She was a large woman, not obese but tall and broad. *They certainly found the right woman for the job.* I thought as she drew me to her bosom and placed the bottle between my lips. I felt engulfed in her arms, which was strangely calming. I suckled tentatively. I tasted the protein shake, vanilla bean. As soon as I started drinking it down, I realized how hungry I was and drank faster. It had been far too long since I had last eaten anything.

"That's a good girl," Deborah cooed. "What a hungry baby you are!" She began rocking me back and forth and humming a lullaby. I had expected to hate it, or at the very least to barely tolerate it, but to my surprise, it was incredibly soothing. My eyes began to grow heavy, and my suckling came slower and slower. I'm not sure if it was the exhaustion or if there was some sedative in that protein shake. Either way, I was drifting off to sleep in Nanny's warm embrace before I could even finish my bottle.

Chapter 3

I'm not sure how long I slept, but it was daylight when I woke up. I was still a bit groggy, but overall I felt much better after a good night's sleep. Someone had placed the pacifier in my mouth after I fell asleep and I spit it out, rolling my eyes. I stretched and shifted in the narrow twin bed to find that my diaper was moist and squishy between my legs. The smell of stale urine wafted up as I moved, verifying that I had wet my pants in the night. I groaned, burning with humiliation. I couldn't believe that I had peed my pants like a baby! They must have sedated me, that is the only way I could have wet myself without realizing it.

The lock slid open, and Deborah came right on in without knocking or even announcing herself. In my embarrassment, I quickly pulled the covers up to hide my puffy diaper, not wanting her to know that I had wet myself in the night. It was futile, however, as the very first thing that she did was to pull the covers right off of me and immediately begin feeling the front of my diaper. I blushed and turned my head toward the wall, sure that I was about to get a lecture of some kind.

"Oooh, it looks like somebody has a full diaper," she cooed.

"That's a good girl. It looks like I'll have to change you," she said. She began to hum a little tune as she reached into the nightstand and pulled out wipes, baby powder, and another diaper. I was confused. This was not quite the reaction I was expecting. She seemed pleased that I had dirtied my diaper for some reason.

"Change me?" I asked, shocked by her words.

"Of course. Babies can't clean themselves up; that's what they need Nannies for," she replied as though it was the most natural thing in the world.

Oh right, the whole age regression thing, that had sort of slipped my mind. I needed coffee, but something told me that wasn't going to be on the breakfast menu. I was willing to play along to some degree in the interest of speeding things along and possibly even getting released early, but having some strange woman be so involved in my bodily functions was a bridge too far.

"Look here -" I began, ready to give her an earful but the cheeky bitch just shoved the pacifier back into my mouth and got on with it. I sulked but decided once again that the consequences of putting up a fight were likely worse than just going along with it.

She pulled the soggy, soiled diaper away and began to clean me up with baby wipes. I would never have admitted it in a thousand years, but it felt very nice to have the stale, sticky urine cleaned away. The baby wipe was soft and sensual against my sensitive areas, and her perfunctory, efficient movements put me at ease. A little bit of powder, and before I knew it, I had a fresh, clean diaper on. This woman knew her way around a diaper change. I had to give her that.

"Now, who's ready for breakfast?" she said her in her best baby voice. I screwed up my face into a grimace, ready to throw a tantrum. I was too hungry for another protein shake. I wanted real food, damn it. To my relief, Sam came in just then with a tray of oatmeal. Not my favorite breakfast, admittedly. I would have preferred a big greasy breakfast of bacon, eggs, and buttered toast. But, under the circumstances, I was just happy to have solid food. He was also dragging an oversized high chair behind him which Nanny took from him and began to set up.

"What is that?" I asked, looking at it uncertainly. Surely they didn't expect -

"Hush," Nanny cut off the thought before I could even finish it.

"Babies can't be expected to feed themselves, now can they?" She said.

"But -" I stopped short as Sam loomed over me, silently daring me to misbehave. My still sore ankle reminded me that I probably should not protest too much. He picked me up and put me in the chair, and Deborah put an adult-sized bib on me. She spoon-fed me oatmeal while cooing and babbling at me like I was a tiny baby. Thankfully, Sam did not stay to watch. He lumbered off to whatever it was that he did when he wasn't bullying young women into high chairs.

Despite my skepticism, I found myself surprised by my response. Being fed was a lot more fun than eating breakfast on my own, and I caught myself caught up in Deborah's choo-choo train game more than once. This age regression therapy was disarmingly powerful. The more that they treated me like a small child, the more normal and natural it felt to act like one.

After breakfast, Deborah announced that I was going to meet Doctor Franken today and I groaned inwardly. I'd had to talk to endless counselors and psychologists and everything in between during my time in the system. I never found it at all helpful. Still,

I knew the rules of the game pretty well by now. Smile, play along, follow the rules, get released, rinse, repeat. Deborah made a big fuss out of finding a pink dress covered in ruffles for me to put on and even found ruffled socks and a shiny pair of mary janes shoes for me to wear. The dress was so ruffled that you couldn't even tell that I had a diaper on underneath. She brushed my hair into pigtails and topped it all off with a bow before standing back to admire her handiwork.

"The doctor is going to like you," she said with an odd twinkle in her eye. I didn't fully understand what she meant by that, but it did make me blush.

Chapter 4

I soon found myself in a chair just outside of the doctor's office, feeling somewhat nervous and more than a little silly. The outfit that Deborah had picked for me made me feel more like a Victorian doll than a grown woman. I sat on my hands and kicked my feet, a nervous habit I've had ever since I was a little girl. I hoped that this doctor was nice.

"Come in, Molly," beckoned a deep, masculine voice as if on cue.

I walked into the office slowly. Behind the large, wooden desk was a man both younger and more handsome than I would have expected. He was in his early to mid-thirties, perhaps, I've never been very good with ages. He had short brown hair and a well-groomed beard, neither of which showed any signs of gray. There was something comforting about him, something in the way his tweed suit crumpled and the way his wireframe sat at an odd angle on his handsome face that made him seem gentle and approachable. I didn't usually find beards attractive, but it suited him. Out of nowhere, I wondered if his beard would tickle if I kissed him. I blushed and tried to put the thought out of my mind.

He was writing something down as I walked in and his glance up at me turned into a double-take. His sleepy blue eyes suddenly took on a hungry look, taking me in from head to toe as though I were the most fantastic thing since the Grand Canyon. Deborah had been right. The doctor seemed to like me very much, indeed.

"Ms. Molly Banks," he said slowly, letting his pen fall to the desk. The sound seemed to bring him back to reality, and he regained his professional decorum. He cleared his throat and straightened his jacket, then gestured toward the chair opposite his desk.

"Please, sit," he said.

His eyes never left me as I crossed the room and

lowered myself onto the chair. Never able to pass up an opportunity to flirt, I let my knees gape open just wide enough to make him wonder. He coughed again and messed around with the papers on his desk for a moment before he could manage to look me in the eyes.

"How are you getting on so far?" he asked, doing a medium job of keeping his voice steady.

"I guess I'm doing ok," I said in a small voice.

"It has been a weird day if I'm honest," I replied. He nodded sympathetically and smiled.

He has such a charming smile, I thought dreamily.

"I know that age regression therapy can seem a bit strange at first, but I promise you that if you keep an open mind, you will be astonished at how quickly you can make progress. How are you adjusting to your diaper?" He asked. I'd forgotten all about that for a moment. I blushed deeply and clamped my legs shut, suddenly feeling like an idiot for trying to flirt while wearing a diaper.

"Um … " I stammered. He chuckled at my embarrassment, which only deepened my humiliation.

"Don't worry. That will take some adjusting to as well. I encourage you to use it as often as you can. In fact, for the first few days at least, it will be a requirement. It does help to put you in the correct mindset. And, on that note, after this initial consultation, you will no longer refer to me as Doctor Franken. From henceforth, you will call me 'Daddy.'" He waited and looked at me, expectantly.

"You want me to call you, Daddy? You can't be serious," I scowled at him.

"I am very serious, young lady, and you can wipe that pout off of your face right now. I allow no brattiness here. You see, I represent a father figure for my patients, something many of them lacked growing up. By bringing you into a regressed state of mind and providing you with that positive father figure while in that state, we hope to train away all of that naughty behavior you've been engaged in recently," he explained. I frowned but resisted the urge to argue, sensing that it would get me nowhere or worse.

"Ok, if you insist," I pouted.

"I do insist. Furthermore, you will refer to Nurse Roberts as 'Nanny,'" he added.

"Who, Deborah?" I asked, guessing that was who he meant.

"No, no," he wagged a finger, reproachfully, "Not Deborah. *Nanny.*"

"Right. Nanny," I said, playing along.

"And I am?" he leaned forward eagerly in his chair. I could almost taste how badly he needed to hear it. Something about that eagerness excited me. I looked down shyly at my lap before looking up at him through a veil of lashes.

"Daddy," I said the words so softly that I was almost speaking in a whisper. He nodded and closed his eyes, savoring it. I wondered if he reacted this was to all of his patients and thought sent a little stab of jealousy through me.

Careful, Molly. This is not a guy you need to be crushing on, I thought to myself.

"Good girl," he said, somewhat shakily.

"Now, that's enough grown-up talk. I believe that Nanny has coloring books and juice waiting for you back in your room. Run along now," he said. I grinned to myself as I walked back to my room, thinking of how flustered he had gotten when I called him "Daddy." I knew how much that had turned him on, and I had no qualms about using that attraction to get what I wanted, an early release. I was so sure that I had him eating out of the palm of my hand, but I had no idea just how wrong I really was.

Chapter 5

"No, little girls go pee-pee in their diapers, not in the toilet!" Nanny cried exasperated. It was late that afternoon, and I was refusing to wet my diaper.

"Please, Nanny, I have to go so bad!" I hopped from foot to foot and squirmed, but the urge to urinate was uncomfortably strong no matter what I did.

"Then go in your diaper!" She crossed her arms and looked at me expectantly.

"Well?" She questioned. I burst into tears. I couldn't do it no matter how hard I tried. Nanny made an irritated noise and grabbed me by the hand, dragging me out of my room and down the hall. Some small part of me realized how ridiculous I must have looked: my bow was crooked, my face was red, and my eyes were swollen from crying. The rest of me couldn't care less, though. I was too upset at being in trouble. After a few short days of coloring, storytime, and naptime, I was already in a deeply regressed state of mind. The cynical brat who had arrived at the Institute was gone. I truly wanted to be the good little girl they expected me to be. I couldn't get over this last hurdle. Nanny marched me straight into Daddy's office. Daddy put down the book he was reading at looked at us with a perplexed look on his face.

"What's going on here?" he asked, a hint of annoyance in his voice from the interruption.

"Well, go on and tell him," Nanny said firmly, giving me a gentle push towards Daddy's desk. I tried to get the words out without crying but failed.

"I can't pee in my diaper," I wailed and buried my face in my hands to hide my shame.

"Oh dear," I heard Nanny tutt quietly behind me. I could sense their disappointment, and it made me want to be swallowed up by the Earth and die.

"Molly," Daddy said gently.

"Look at me," he added. I brought my hands down just low enough to meet his gaze.

"I told you that you would have to use your diaper for the first few days, remember? If you don't go tinkle in your diaper, I'm afraid that you'll have to be punished. You don't want that, do you?" He asked. I shook my head silently, my bottom lip quivering.

"Good. Now be a brave girl for Daddy and use your diaper, ok?" His soothing voice said. I gave it one last shot, but no matter how I tried, not even a drop came out. Daddy sighed with disappointment.

"Okay, little one, if that's the way it's going to be. I want you to know that this will hurt me a lot more than it hurts you," he said. His eyes told me his words where true. Nanny led me over to his desk, my face still streaming with tears, wondering what he was going to do to me, fearing the worst. He pulled me onto his lap, face down, and pulled up my skirt. Before I even had a chance to react, he whacked my diapered bottom with his hand, very hard. I froze with fear and pain, too shocked to even cry. Over and over, he brought his hand firmly onto my rear end without mercy. Even though the padding of the diaper, every blow stung more than the last. The pain and humiliation were overwhelming, and, after the initial shock wore off, I began to sob. I sobbed and squirmed and kicked my legs but Daddy just held me tighter and didn't relent. He methodically covered every square inch of my bottom with blows. As much as it hurt, as much as I wanted him to stop, I couldn't help but notice that my body was also humming with arousal. That made me feel even more ashamed of myself, and I cried even harder. At last, I was so overwhelmed that I was finally able to pee.

Once it began, it all came flooding out of me, and I completely soaked my diaper. The spanking stopped, and Daddy patted the back of my diaper approvingly. He held me close, patting my puffing diaper and rocking me until I stopped crying.

"It's ok, sweetie," he would occasionally

mutter.

"Let it all out. Cry as much as you need to. Daddy is here. So is Nanny. You're ok. Everything is alright," his words were soothing, and his embrace was warm. I relaxed into him, forgetting all about the pain and the shame, enjoying the feeling of being held. I felt so safe there. When my sniffling finally stopped, he gave me one last firm squeeze on the butt before telling me to stand up. My legs were wobbly, but I managed to stay upright as he inspected me. He reached under my skirt and felt the puffy swell of my diaper, patting it with satisfaction. To be sure, he pulled on the elastic waistband and inspected me visually as well.

"Good girl," he muttered as he looked at me.

"You were such a good girl, taking your spanking so well. I'm very proud of you for using your diaper," he said. It was as if his eyes burned right into me and I couldn't help but feel proud of myself when he said those words, even though a small part of me was still mortified that I had just peed my pants. The doctor had worked up a light sweat from spanking me. He pulled a handkerchief from his jacket pocket and dabbed at his forehead as he regained his composure.

"Take her to get cleaned up," he instructed Nanny.

"And make sure she is properly shaved at once," he said before we left the room.

Chapter 6

To my surprise, Nanny didn't take me back to my room or to the communal showers, but rather to a private bathroom. It was considerably more beautiful, with a huge clawfoot bathtub, scented candles along the rim, and an assortment of bath toys waiting in a basket on the floor. Nanny drew some warm water, sprinkled in a few bubbles, and removed my pretty, ruffled dress and soggy diaper.

"Good girls get bubble baths," she cooed as she helped me in.

"And you've been a perfect girl," she added. Now that I had submitted to their wishes and peed in my diaper, she was as cheerful as the sunshine, humming a little tune as she scrubbed my body thoroughly. She gave me a few toys to play with as she washed my hair, and I lost myself in a cute little game of sink the ducky. The warm water was relaxing, and Nanny's fingers on my scalp felt like a lovely massage. She had me lean back as she poured bathwater over my hair, rinsing all the suds away until I was squeaky clean. All too soon, bath time was over, and Nanny had me on my bed with my legs in the air, ready to be shaved. She covered me with shaving cream and set about the task of shaving me, which she did with military precision. Her touch felt more maternal than sexual, and I relaxed into the pleasant sensations of having my vagina shaved by somebody else. I usually do the task myself, and it was only a few days overdue, so Nanny was able to make quick work of it. It was quite lovely to be pampered after such an emotionally draining day, almost like what I imagined a spa day would be like. With expert precision, Nanny applied the powder and a fresh diaper, giving me a little boop on the nose when she was done.

"I imagine that you're ready for bed little one," she said in a sweet voice as she pulled my nightgown down over my head.

"You have had a massive day today. Nanny is very proud of you," she said, making me smile. Her words made me blush. It was barely dark outside, but she was right. I was exhausted! The thought of curling up against Nanny's bosom as she fed me a bottle sounded delightful. She had Sam bring in a fresh bottle and rocked me gently as I suckled on it. As I sucked it down, she told me a story about a pretty princess who was kidnapped by a mean old dragon and taken away to live in his evil kingdom. The good knight fought his way over treacherous mountains and dangerous deserts on his way to rescue her. I fell asleep somewhere between the dragon-slaying and true love's kiss.

***

Bill watched the woman go, her wet diaper making her ruffled dress puff out behind her. He normally didn't let his tendencies affect his job, but this young lady was having an unusual effect on him. She was so beautiful but also very vulnerable and eager to please. She had taken to the age regression therapy quicker than most and was already using her diaper.

That doesn't make her a little, Bill warned himself. *Don't get your hopes up,* he said to himself. Being a Daddy was hard sometimes. His job as a counselor was gratifying, and there were indeed similarities to the lifestyle, but it wasn't the same. He longed for a real relationship, a baby girl that he could call his very own. Most of the women he'd dated were varying levels of disinterested or disgusted by his affinity. On the rare occasions when he had met a woman who shared them, they had turned out to be incompatible in other areas. Bill sighed heavily, suddenly feeling very lonely. He wanted to take Molly home, dress her up in the prettiest dresses, buy her all the toys her heart desired, and snuggle up next to her every night.

You're dreaming. She's a patient. She isn't interested in you. She doesn't want you creeping on her. But the way she called him Daddy on her first day here, breathless and excited, wouldn't let him give up hope entirely. The memory made his cock throb. So too, did the recent events. It felt delicious to spank her and check her diaper. At that moment, he had done his best to maintain a clinical detachment. Now, alone, the memory was driving him wild. He got up and locked the door to his office. Sure that he wouldn't be disturbed, he kicked off his trousers, taking his erection in hand. In his mind's eye, he saw Molly kneeling before him clad only in a diaper and little white bows on her pigtails. She was playing with her nipples as she watched him stroke himself.

"Want some help with that, Daddy?" asked his fantasy.

"Yes, baby girl," she lovingly said. She wrapped her warm, soft lips around him, sucking him like a lollipop. He moaned as her little pink tongue worked its way up to his shaft. She gently cupped his balls and smiled up at him with the face of an angel.

"Cum for me, Daddy. Cum all over my face!"

He obliged her, and she giggled as he showered her with his love.

That's better, he thought, feeling a bit more clear-headed.

You really shouldn't be thinking of a patient like that, anyway. He quickly cleaned up his mess and unlocked the door. Thoughts of Molly still lingered in his mind, however. He wasn't able to shake them, no matter how he tried to distract himself or tell himself that she was out of bounds.

Chapter 7

The next day started much the same as all the others had, only this time when the smell of urine and the squishy diaper between my legs made it clear that I had wet my diaper again, I was relieved instead of ashamed, knowing how proud of me Daddy and Nanny would be. Sure enough, Nanny was full of praise for me when she saw how full my diaper had gotten overnight. She even gave me a strawberry sticker to play with as she cleaned me up and put a fresh, clean diaper on me. The soft material of the diaper rubbed against my freshly shaved vagina in the most exhilarating way. As a familiar tingle came over me, I thought back to the hungry way Daddy had looked at me, and the tingle only got stronger.

Nanny announced during breakfast that today's treatment would be just before lunch. I smiled and squirmed in my highchair, eager to find out what the doctor might have in store for me today. The morning seemed to drag on, but Nanny finally announced that it was time for my treatment. As I walked to Daddy's office, I began to feel a little bit nervous, remembering the day before. What if he spanked me again? It wasn't that painful, it had even stirred some pleasant feeling in me, but the thought of going through it still filled me with dread. What was it about it that scared me so? Then, it hit me. It was his anger that I feared, not the spanking itself. I didn't want to disappoint him.

Daddy was waiting for me in the middle of his office. A fluffy purple blanket spread out at his feet. He looked very handsome in his tweed jacket and neatly trimmed beard. As he smiled at me, I felt my insides clench with excitement.

"Good morning, princess," he greeted me as I came in.

"Nanny tells me that you've been a very good girl for her this morning. I'm very proud of you," he said. I blushed and looked at the floor, overwhelmed by the emotions that he made me feel, but also embarrassed that his opinion carried so much weight with me. After so many years of cynically rebelling against authority, craving approval felt a bit strange. The doctor continued.

"You've made excellent progress in your regression. Today, I want you to go a little bit deeper. The deeper into regression we can take you, the more the positive messages will be able to implant into your subconscious. I thought we might start with some tummy time," his said, clapping his hands together.

"What the fuck is tummy time?" As soon as the word left my mouth, I knew I was in trouble. Daddy's eyes narrowed, and his voice grew cold.

"What did you just say?" he snapped. I gasped and covered my mouth with both hands, but it was already too late. I couldn't believe it. Here I was supposed to be putting myself in the mind frame of a little girl, and before I could stop myself, the dirtiest word of them all had come flying out of my mouth. Hot tears welled up behind my eyes. I honestly was a bad girl. Despite his tightly controlled exterior, his anger and disappointment were palpable.

"That is a no-no word! You know what happens now, little one?" I shook my head. My hands still clamped over my mouth.

"You're getting your mouth washed out with soap," he ordered. Before I could react, he was dragging me by the hand to his private washroom attached to his office. He turned the water on in the sink and pulled my hand away from my mouth. Squirting a tiny amount of hand soap onto his index finger, he turned to face me.

"Open," he commanded. I could already feel the stinging in my eyes and knew that tears wouldn't be far behind if he would just let me explain.

"Daddy, please -" Before I could get another word out, his finger was in my mouth. The soap tasted terrible, and he rubbed it all over my tongue and teeth.

"This will teach you never to talk like that again. That kind of filthy language does not belong in the mouth of little girls, do you hear me?" He barked. I nodded and burst into tears. His anger was too much for me to handle. At the sight of my tears, he softened a bit.

"Alright, little one, rinse out your mouth," he said. He held my hair back as I bent over the sink, cupping the water into my mouth and ordering me to spit it out until the taste of soap began to fade away. When I was done, he gently dried my red-splotchy face off with a hand towel. I must have been a sad sight indeed my swollen eyes and damp dress because he picked me up as though I weighed nothing at all and carried me back into his office. Still cradling me against his chest, he sat in one of the chairs and wrapped his arms around me tightly, burying his face in the top of my head with a sigh.

"I'm so sorry that I made you mad, Daddy," I said, rubbing my eyes.

"Do you forgive me?" I asked, my little voice

quiet against his chest.

"Daddy isn't mad at you anymore, sweetheart. And I'm sorry that I had to punish you like that, but it's important for you to learn how to behave like a good little girl. It's my job to teach you right from wrong, and if I don't do that, I can't be a good Daddy to you. Do you understand?" He explained. I nodded and sniffled. He put his finger under my chin, gently raising my face to meet his own.

"Look at me, little one," he said. With big, watery eyes, I met his baby blue gaze.

"Of course, I forgive you. There is nothing that you could ever do that I couldn't forgive. I might have to punish you from time to time but don't ever think for even one minute that it means that you're not my princess anymore," he said. He pulled me close, and I closed my eyes, relaxing into his warm embrace. He petted my hair and kissed my forehead until my tears finally stopped.

"There's my brave girl," he said gently, wiping

my nose with his handkerchief.

"Now, let me see you smile," he said.

I managed a tiny, shaky smile, but Daddy wasn't satisfied with that. He tickled my sides and underarms until I shook with laughter and squirmed to get away, the sound of my giggles filling his small office.

"That's better," he said and pulled me close to him once again. I could feel the hardness that had grown in his lap, and instinctively I squirmed against it. He inhaled sharply as my padded bottom made contact with his erection. I bit my lip, blushed, and looked away as if it were an accident.

"Well, I think that's enough time for today, little one," he said abruptly, standing up and walking me briskly to the door. He paused before closing the door behind him.

"You did very well today. I'm proud of you," he said.

Something about the way he said it, his voice warm and soft, made me tingle in my diaper again. I thought about how hard he had gotten when I giggled and squirmed in his lap. It was apparent that he wanted me, but he had cut our session short just when things were starting to get juicy. Had I done something wrong? On the other hand, he had said that he was proud of me just before I left, so that was confusing. I decided not to worry too much about and skipped down the hall back to my room where Nanny would be waiting with cookies and juice.

***

That evening, Bill couldn't manage to sleep no matter how hard he tried. He couldn't get Molly out of his head. It didn't matter how many times he masturbated, thoughts of her were never far behind.

This was more than just sexual attraction, he realized. He wanted to hold her, to talk to her, to protect her. A sweet thing like her needed protection. She should have someone watching over her, keeping her safe. Sadly, she had no one at all. She was all alone in the world, and it broke Bill's heart.

He sighed and turned over onto his side, punching his pillow to try to reshape it. He shouldn't be having these thoughts, he knew. He should be focused on her recovery, on getting her healthy, on helping her get over her past. Her life story read like a horror novel, losing her parents suddenly in a car crash at a very young age, passed from foster home to foster home, kicked out at eighteen when the government's money dried up. He cursed the sorry excuses for foster parents she had been subjected to. She deserved so much better. You would have never known that she had lived through so much just by talking to her.

How could someone who had lived through so much pain be so sweet? He thought.

Most patients lashed out in cruel ways during their recovery. It was only human nature. Molly, however, never had. Yes, she had thrown temper tantrums, but never once did he hear her say one cruel word to him or Nurse Roberts. Not only was she beautiful and vulnerable, but she was also sweet and submissive. She deserved to be cherished, to be somebody's baby girl.

Not mine, he thought, his heart aching.

Stop thinking of her like that. You're a professional. It didn't matter how many times he said it, thoughts of her ran through his mind unbidden.

I need a break, he thought.

I need a chance to clear my head, to get her off my mind. He decided that he would cancel her treatment tomorrow. It was better to fall one day behind on their progress than to risk doing something inappropriate. He flashed back to the moment earlier in the day when she had innocently brushed against his reaction and blushed.

What a pervert she must think I am! He couldn't shake the feeling that she was attracted to him as well. The way she looked at him seemed to hang on his every word. If that were true, it would only make things worse. He would never be able to resist her if she wanted him as well. He groaned and rolled over again. Yes, some space would be wise.

Chapter 8

That evening, I didn't go down when Nanny gave me a bottle like I usually did. I couldn't stop thinking about Daddy and the special tingles he gave me. As Nanny tiptoed out of the room, thinking I was asleep, I began to squirm in my fresh diaper, letting the silky material rub against me. With a glance at the door, I snaked my hand down the elastic band of my diaper. The light dusting of baby powder made my freshly shaved skin feel silky-smooth against my fingertips. As my fingers found my magic button, my eyes fluttered closed, and I thought of Daddy. His big, strong hands wrapped around me, holding me close. The way his pants bulged every time he saw me, the hungry look in his eyes. I knew that he wanted me, and it drove me crazy. Being desired was a powerful aphrodisiac for me, and his lust was setting me on fire. I reached under my frilly pink nightgown and groped my tiny breasts, pinching the pert pink buds until they stood rigidly at attention. I thought of all the cute nicknames he had for me, *princess* and *little one*, and how special they made me feel. In my mind, I could hear him telling me what a good girl I was and how proud he was of me, over and over, until I was shivering with pleasure. I hesitated before allowing myself to climax, however. Whenever I orgasmed, it made a huge mess, gushing out of me in waves. Usually, that wasn't a problem because my underwear wasn't being inspected every morning under usual circumstances. On the other hand, I desperately needed to relieve some tension if I had any hope of getting to sleep.

If I wet my diaper, Nanny will never notice, I suddenly realized. I smiled and went back to rubbing my magic button, imagining that it was Daddy's hands, not mine, guiding me gently but firmly to an earth-shattering orgasm. I bit my lip so as not to cry out and let it all come rushing out of me, flooding my diaper with my slick juices. For a long moment, all I could do was take shaky, rapid breaths, and try not to moan out loud. After a while, I came back to myself. Should I wait to see if I would wet my pants overnight? I decided it was best not to take the chance. Some things are better left private. I had a faint urge to go, and it took some coaxing to come out. I was still adjusting to using a diaper to pee, especially when lying down. Nanny assured me that with more practice, it would become more comfortable and easier, but I was still struggling. I bore down harder and managed a small sprinkle, adding to my already soggy diaper. It was a warm and soothing sensation, and before long, I was fast asleep.

Chapter 9

Nanny didn't notice anything unusual about my diaper the next morning, other than to remark that it seemed extra full. This earned me lots of praise and a banana sticker to add to my growing collection. I played with it gleefully as she cleaned me up and put a fresh, clean diaper on me.

All morning, I looked forward to my next treatment with the doctor, but Nanny never did take me. By the time lunch rolled by, I had begun to worry that I wouldn't see him that day, but I did my best to put the thought out of my head. When nap time came and went, I was feeling downright distraught. What had I done wrong? Did he hate me and never want to see me again? It may sound irrational, but in my regressed state of mind, it was the only possible explanation. I was a bad girl, and he didn't want to be my Daddy anymore. The thought put me in a terrible mood, and I refused to cooperate with Nanny on any front. I wouldn't color or sit still for storytime. I threw my afternoon snack on the floor. The age regression therapy had done its job very well, and I was no longer able to express my anger and frustration like an adult would. I was no longer capable of saying, "Nanny, I would like to see the doctor now, please. I think treatment would do me good." I could only throw my cheerios in the poor woman's face and hope that she somehow got the message.

"That's it!" she finally snapped. "I'm afraid I'm going to have to tell your Daddy on you, young lady!" she exclaimed. I froze with fear. I had wanted his attention so badly that I didn't think about what that would mean if it was in response to a tantrum. I immediately burst into tears. He would be so angry with me! Desperately, I begged and pleaded with Nanny not to tell on me. I promised to be a good girl and to go to bed early, anything to win my way back into her good graces. Nanny had no sympathy for me. I had successfully pushed her well beyond her limit. She dragged me right down the hallway and made me wait outside while she told Daddy every horrible thing that I had done to her that day. I sobbed and wailed as I waited, beyond caring who saw or heard me and what they might think. After a few minutes, Nanny stepped out and informed me that Daddy would like to see me in his office right away. I obeyed, tears still streaming down my face. Daddy watched silently as I crossed his office slowly; my vision still somewhat blurred. Once I was settled in a chair, he leaned down and gently wiped my face with his handkerchief before commanding me to blow my nose into it. His tone told me that he was in no mood for backtalk, so I complied. He wiped my nose gingerly before folding up his hanky into a neat square and placing it back in his jacket pocket.

"Now I want you to stop this nonsense right away. Nanny says that you have been terrorizing her all day. What could have possibly gotten into you?" he asked sternly.

"You were doing so well," he added. I tried to find the words to explain that I was confused and afraid and lonely but failed. Another wave of tears threatened to come up, but I managed to barely hold them back with a trembling lip. I looked at him with watery eyes, silently begging him not to be angry with me. Daddy sighed and took off his glasses.

"I know this has been a big week for you, little one. You've had a lot to adjust to, right?" He said. I nodded and sniffed. He squatted down so that we were eye-level.

"Listen to me, sweetheart. You can't go around throwing temper tantrums every time you don't get what you want. This is a very critical time for your therapy. We have reached the stage in your development where you need to learn to ask for what you want," he explained. I looked at him, wide-eyed, his words not registering in my regressed state of mind.

"I need you to use your words like a big girl," he elaborated, his velvety voice was like a warm blanket wrapped around me, keeping me safe.

"What made you so upset today pumpkin?" He asked. He put his hand on my knee and looked at me with those deep blue eyes and it finally all came rushing out of me.

"I wanted to see you, but Nanny didn't bring me down for my treatment, and I got scared that you didn't want to see me and maybe I did something wrong, and you didn't like me anymore," I blurted out. All of this was between great heaving sobs, but I managed to get it all out before dissolving into a total hysterical mess. Daddy picked me up and sat with me in his lap, holding me while I cried.

"There, there," he muttered occasionally as I wept. I completely soaked his tweed jacket with my tears, but at no point did he chastise me or act disgusted. He only held me and stroked my hair, letting me cry as much as I wanted to. Finally, I managed to stop long enough to ask, "A-are you going top-punish me?" He sighed and kissed my forehead, his soft, warm lips lingering on my skin.

"No, little one, I think this one is Daddy's fault," he said. I looked up at him, my head still resting on his shoulder, my brows knitted together in confusion. He smiled down at me and brushed his fingers lightly over my moist cheek, wiping away the tears that still lingered there.

"I should have had an appointment with you today. You are here because you need help. It wasn't fair of me to cancel your treatment just because of my feelings. I'm very sorry. Do you forgive me?" I nodded at him, unable to speak. His fingers brushed over my lips, and for one breathless moment, I thought, hoped, that he might kiss me. The moment passed, however, and he didn't kiss me, much to my disappointment. Instead, he sighed sadly before leading me over to the bookshelf next to his desk. The bottom shelves were filled with picture books and puzzles.

"I think I owe you a little one-on-one time. Pick something out, and we'll do it together," he said. He rested his hand on my shoulder and looked down at me with a warm smile. I suddenly felt like the whole world was glowing, especially me. I considered the options for a moment, then decided that a puzzled would probably take the longest, therefore giving me more time with Daddy. I found the puzzle with the most amount of pieces and handed it to him with a smile. Daddy patiently helped me put the puzzle together. I got a great deal of enjoyment of pretending not to know how to fit it together and the gentle way. Daddy would show me how to do it correctly. Something about the soft way he spoke to me and the affection in his eyes made my heart blossom open. I wanted nothing more than for the afternoon to go on and on forever. Of course, the time passed all too quickly. Daddy announced that he had another appointment to get ready for and I tried not to pout, even though I wanted to.

"I do have something for you before you go, however," he said. He walked over to his desk and pulled something out of the drawer. As he brought it closer, I saw that it was a small silver box. He handed it to me.

"Go on, open it," he encouraged. I looked at his shining face for a moment before I gently pried the lid open. Inside, nestled in velvet lining, was a silver pacifier with "Daddy's Girl" engraved into it. I picked it up reverently to find that it was a functioning pacifier with a rubber tip and everything. I put it hastily in my mouth and grinned.

"You look beautiful, honey," he said. Then, he leaned down and kissed my pacifier.

"Run along now, Daddy will see you tomorrow," he said as I left. My heart was all aflutter. He had kissed me! Well, sort of. As I walked into the lobby, I saw another young lady, all dressed in ribbons and bows. When she saw my pacifier, she screwed up her face in anger.

Eat your heart out, I thought, somewhat ungenerously, and skipped happily back to my room.

***

As Molly left, Bill finally admitted that something had to be done. She was pretty clearly reciprocating his feelings. He knew that he wouldn't be able to resist her charms forever, not when he knew that she wanted him as well. He also knew that nothing could happen between them while she was under his care. He went to Molly's file and opened it, seeking out the name of the judge who had sentenced her. Surely, there was a reasonable solution to be found.

Chapter 10

The next several days passed uneventfully. I stopped counting the days until my release and began to enjoy my time at the Institute. Daddy said I was making excellent progress in my treatments, and I had the sticker collection to prove it. In my sessions, I slowly worked my way up in age, relearning important developmental markers that I had missed the first time around. I learned manners for the very first time, as well as the importance of being kind to others. Growing up in a dog-eat-dog kind of environment, this was a whole new world for me.

One day, Nanny announced that Daddy had a special surprise for me. A herd of butterflies instantly flooded my stomach. He had not outwardly shown any attraction to me in our recent sessions, but I knew it was still there. Every day I waited and hoped that today would be the day that he cracked and swept me off my feet, but it never happened. I tried looking as adorable and irresistible as I could, but still nothing.

What if today is the day? I wondered before pushing the thought out of my mind. Best not to get your hopes up in matters of romance as I had learned the hard way. Almost every crush I had ever had culminated in a half-drunk hump in the back of somebody's car.

Nanny had laid out some clothes for me, jeans and a beautiful blouse, very different from the frills and bows she usually dressed me in. Big girl clothes, as I had come to think of them. As I put them on, I began to feel closer to myself than I had felt in weeks. At the same time, I knew that I was different, healthier, and more confident. It felt good.

"My little girl is growing up," Nanny said as she watched me dress, dabbing a tear from her eye. I almost laughed at what I thought was a corny joke when I noticed that both the tears and the emotions were real.

"Oh Nanny," I said, quickly crossing the room for a hug.

"I'll always be your little girl," I said, almost involuntarily. I meant it, too. When I first arrived, she had seemed so cold and stern, but now I thought of her as the grandmother I'd never had. Embarrassed by the show of emotion, I stepped back and looked into the small mirror hanging above my bed.

"How do I look?" I asked, unable to see below my shoulders in the small mirror.

"Beautiful," Nanny said, tearing up again, "Absolutely beautiful." This time I did laugh, hoping to cheer her up a bit.

"Ha! You have to say that, you're my Nanny," I said playfully. She managed a weak, watery smile before shooing me off to my appointment.

Rather than waiting for me in his office, as he usually did, Daddy was waiting for me in the lobby with his coat in hand. He was twirling his car keys on his finger and rocking back and forth on his heels. I wondered what had made him so happy.

"Hello, pumpkin," he greeted me with a happy smile.

"I thought we might go out for some ice cream, what do you say?" He asked with his handsome grin. I was so overcome with happiness that I couldn't say anything. I could only jump for joy and squeal with delight. Daddy threw his head back and laughed.

"I'll take that as a 'yes,'" he said and offered me his arm. I took it with a smile, and he led me outside to his car. It was the first time I had been outside in weeks. The bright sun made me squint a bit, but I was happy to be out in it nonetheless. The parking lot that had once seemed so dinky to me now seemed alive with flowering trees and singing birds. I even saw a couple of squirrels playing in the grass which I excitedly pointed out to Daddy. I wasn't sure if it was the oncoming spring or a change in my outlook, but everything looked so fresh to me suddenly, more alive. As we drove to the ice cream shop, I chatted happily about everything I saw out of the passenger side window and all the things I couldn't wait to do when I was done with treatment. The age regression had brought me out of my shell, and I no longer second-guessed every word out of my mouth, worrying if people would suddenly stop liking me. Daddy had assured me and reassured me on many occasions that I was a smart and funny young woman and that the world was lucky to hear as many of my thoughts as possible. I was so grateful to him for everything that he had done for me. We pulled into the ice cream store, and I excitedly grabbed for the handle, ready to bound out of the car, but Daddy put a hand on my arm to stop me.

"No, wait here a moment," he said kindly but firmly. We may have left the facility, but it was clear who was still in charge, something I found both comforting and thrilling. He got out and walked over to my side of the car, opening the door and extending his hand to me to help me out. I took it, somewhat breathlessly, feeling like the most pampered princess in all the land. The way he put his hand on the small of my back as he opened the door of the shop, guiding me inside, almost made me swoon. Once inside, I had some trouble picking a flavor. There were so many choices! Daddy let me try as many samples as I wanted, patiently allowing me to narrow down the options until I finally settled on a double scoop of chocolate ripple fudge on a waffle cone. Daddy only got a single scoop of plain chocolate. We found a quiet corner of the shop where we could sit and eat our ice cream in private.

"Thank you for the ice cream, Daddy," I said. It had been a long time since anyone had bought me anything, even something as simple as an ice cream cone.

"You can call me Bill if you want," he said.

"You know ... since we're not at the facility right now and all," he said.

"Oh," I said, slowly, not sure how I felt about that.

"Well, do you mind if I still call you, Daddy?" I asked, smiling as his face lit up.

"Not at all. I rather like it, actually," he replied. He blushed a little when he said that and suddenly, we were no longer doctor and patient, we were just Bill and Molly, sharing an ice cream cone on a lovely day out. I liked seeing him blush. It was kind of nice to think that I might make him get butterflies in his tummy the same way that he did to me.

"Cool," I said with a grin.

"I like it too," he replied. We ate our ice cream in contented silence for a moment. It was nice to be with someone without feeling the need to continually impress them or entertain them.

"There was a reason I wanted to get you out of the office today. I have some fantastic news," he said after a time.

"Oh!" I said excitedly, my mind racing. I tried not to fidget or squirm in my seat, so I nodded encouragingly instead.

"What is it?" I curiously asked.

"I've spoken to the judge about you. We are

both very impressed by the progress you have made, and we both feel that you were the product of unfortunate circumstances. I told him that you deserve a second chance, and he agreed. The judge has agreed to release you early on probationary status," he said.

"Yay!" I squealed. At last, I had my freedom back. Then my joy quickly died. If I had gotten this news last week, I would have been ecstatic. All I had wanted since my arrival was an early release. Now, it dawned on me that it would mean leaving behind all the things I had come to love about the facility, including Daddy and Nanny. *No wonder Nanny was so emotional earlier,* I realized, caught somewhat off guard by the heartache that the thought inspired. I wasn't so sure that I was ready to leave them behind.

"What's wrong?" asked Daddy, putting his comfortingly large hand over mine, sensing the sudden shift in my mood.

"Well, technically, I'm kind of homeless. I don't have anywhere to go," I admitted. I was more than a little embarrassed, feeling like a total loser.

"I was going to mention, and no pressure or anything, of course. But I do have a spare room you could stay in until you find a place to stay," he said. He almost winced when he said it. He seemed so nervous that I would say no. When I squealed and danced in my chair, he perked back up again. God, he was just the cutest thing.

"Thank you, thank you, thank you," I gushed.

"I promise, I'll be a perfect roommate, and I swear not to overstay my welcome," I quickly added.

"Oh, I'm not worried about that," he said, giving my hand another firm squeeze. We went back to the institute to get my things. I didn't have many possessions, just a few changes of clothes. Nanny tearfully told me that she had added a few additional outfits for me as she handed me a duffle bag packed to overflowing. At the sight of it, I started tearing up as well, and soon we were hugging one another and blubbering. Bill tried awkwardly but gently to comfort us both.

"There, there. You're only moving a few miles up the road, Molly. We can have Nanny over for dinner any time you both like. Won't that be nice?" He offered. It was a comforting thought. Nanny wiped my face with a hanky and sent me off with a kiss on the forehead. Bill wrapped his arm around my shoulder as we walked to the car, which lifted my spirits tremendously. Soon, I was buckled into the passenger seat of Daddy's car, holding his hand as we drove out of the gates of the Institute and towards our new life together.

Chapter 11

Bill lived in a small ranch style house. The interior was sparsely decorated, but the whole place was obsessively neat. There was a couch and a TV in the living room and a table in the kitchen and not much else. He showed me to the guest room, which had a futon hastily stashed in the corner and a small nightstand. It was pretty similar to my room at the Institute.

"We can fix it up however you like," he said, putting the duffle bag down on the futon.

"I'll take you wherever you like this weekend to get decorations or and anything else you'd like. Sorry about the futon. It was the best I could get on short notice," he said.

He went out and bought that specifically for me, I thought and blushed deeply.

"I love it," I said and smiled at him, hoping

that he would know how sincere I was. Maybe some people would turn their noses up at a brand-new futon, but after a lifetime of sharing beds with foster siblings and, more recently, couch surfing, it was wonderful to have a space of my very own. His face lit up, and he took my hand in his, warm and strong.

"Really? I want you to be comfortable here. Maybe, in time, you will come to think of this as your home," he said. The thought filled me with such warmth that all I could do was grin at him and blush again. We looked at each other for a moment, hand in hand. Was this the moment when he would finally kiss me? He lifted my hand and kissed the back of it, tenderly, while continuing to look into my eyes. I felt my breath catch as his lips touched me, a surge of adrenaline flooding my body. Taking that as an invitation, he pulled me closer and cupped my face with his hand. His body was warm against mine, and I melted into him, my eyes fluttering closed.

"Molly," he whispered. Slowly, he pressed his lips to mine. He kissed me softly, gently at first, waiting for me to blossom open for him before deepening the kiss. As our tongues met, a shock of electricity sent shivers all over my body. All of the longing, all of the aching for him that had been bubbling just under the surface since we met suddenly came rushing to the surface. I made a soft noise of pleasure and ran my fingers through his silky, brown hair. I was ready to rip my clothes off and give myself to him then and there, but he didn't seem to be in any hurry. He explored my mouth slowly, savoring every detail. He broke off the kiss abruptly and smiled at me. I stifled a whimper of longing and neediness, wanting more.

"Well, I'll let you get unpacked. Think you'll be ready for dinner soon?" He asked. I felt hazy like I was in a dream, but I managed to nod and say "yes" and smiled as though every fiber of my being weren't on fire. He kissed me lightly on the forehead and left, closing the door softly behind him. I stood there as if in a daze, burning for him more than ever.

I emerged sometime later, having recovered my wits and unpacked my bags. In addition to some extra clothes, I had discovered that Nanny had snuck some extra toys into my bag and it had taken some time to rank them and find them homes befitting of that rank. As I came into the hall, I was greeted by the most delicious smell. I followed my nose to the kitchen to find the table was already set, complete with candlelight. Bill was still moving things around in pots and pans, but already the aroma was delicious.

"Hey, princess," he greeted me with a smile. I blushed, pleased that he still used his special names with me.

"You have perfect timing. Dinner is almost ready, go ahead, and have a seat," he said.

"What's for dinner?" I asked as he pulled out a chair for me to sit in. I was a bit overwhelmed by all the attention, but I didn't want to show it in case he stopped. Overwhelming or not, I was eating it up.

"Chicken parmigiana," he said, turning back

to the stove.

"I hope you like cheese!" He exclaimed.

"I sure do! Smells delicious," I said enthusiastically. I watched him cook for a moment, impressed at his skill. I could barely make macaroni without burning it. How could a man like that still be single? He had his place, a steady job, and was incredibly good looking. I felt so lucky at that moment, a handsome man cooking for me and a place to call home.

And it's just getting started. I thought as he brought over two plates. He tied a napkin around me like a bib and cut my meal up into little pieces, reminding me to let it cool before tucking into his plate. It was quiet as we ate, something that would have bothered me in the past, but tonight it felt comfortable. Just being around him put him at ease. I got full rather quickly, but I kept eating anyway because it was so delicious! I honestly couldn't remember the last time someone cooked for me, but it had to have been when I was still a kid. Eventually, he slowed down as well, clearly reaching his limits.

"Don't feel as though you have to clean your entire plate, princess?" he said with a wink.

"This is a heavy meal, even for a big guy like me," he said. He patted his belly and winked at me again, making me laugh. I put down my fork, admitting defeat. He was right. The meal was deceptively filling.

"I wanted to talk to you about something," he said, taking my hand from across the table.

"Since we're going to be living together for a while, I feel like I should be as honest with you as possible. You see, I don't just engage in age regression for my job. I also like to engage in age play as a lifestyle as well," he said. He paused as if giving me time to be shocked but of course, I wasn't. I had known this about him from the very beginning.

Did he think he was subtle? I stifled a giggle, not wanting to give him some a complex, and nodded encouragingly.

"Go on," I said.

"I like to nurture and protect; it's just in my nature. It always has been. I don't know why I am this way, but I am, and there is no changing that. Being a Daddy lets me express that side of myself. It has been difficult, especially in terms of finding a woman who can tolerate it. I have yet to meet one who can. But today, at the ice cream store, you said that you would like to keep calling me Daddy. Did you mean it?" He paused and looked at me almost hopefully.

"I did! I love calling you Daddy," I nodded enthusiastically.

"Do you think you'd like to keep being little as well? Not all the time, just when you are in the mood," he asked, making me tilt my head from side to side. I considered it for a moment and realized that it had become a part of me. I loved being little.

"I could keep my sticker collection?" I asked, making him laughed and kissed my hand.

"Yes, you can keep your sticker collection. You can have anything you like, baby girl. Assuming that you want to be my baby girl, that is," he said with a smirk. It was my turn to laugh. The thought of being his filled me with such joy that all I could do is let it spill out of me in ripples.

"Yes, I want that very much," I replied gleefully. He stood and picked me up from my chair, consuming me in a hungry kiss as he held me close.

"Oh, baby," he whispered against my lips.

"My sweet girl," he whispered into the kiss. He carried me to his room and gently laid me down on his bed, my hair fanning around me as he slowly settled his weight on top of me. He stared at me, wide-eyed, as he traced my lips and cheekbones with his fingertips, handling me delicately as though I were some rare work of art.

"You are so beautiful," he whispered.

"Inside and out. I can't believe how lucky I am. I can't get enough of you," he said. Again, he captured my mouth with his. This time the kiss was deep, his tongue insisting on dominance. I happily submitted, allowing him to explore my mouth, my neck, my breasts. He frantically pulled my shirt up, taking a nipple into his mouth and nibbling it lightly. I moaned and ran my fingers through his soft hair as he teased me with his lips, tongue, and teeth. He stopped just long enough to take my clothes off.

"Arms up," he commanded breathlessly and as soon as I obeyed, my shirt was gone. As he unzipped my pants, he saw that I was still wearing my diaper, and he breathed in sharply.

"Baby girl," he exclaimed before placing a gentle kiss just below my belly button.

"You are so perfect," he said. I blushed slightly as his words but inside, I glowed with pride. He peeled my pants off and took a moment to admire me as I lay there in only my diaper. His eyes drank me in as he began to remove his clothing as well. Underneath that tweed suit was a surprisingly toned body. Light brown hair sprinkled his chest and trailed down his washboard abs. Everything about him was so incredibly sexy. As he took his pants off, I noticed that just the sight of me was enough to bring him to full-mast. My diaper was the last to go, and we were finally both fully naked. He settled back on top of me, his hardness nestled between my thighs. I was already slick with desire, and my arousal made me bolder than I usually am. I ran my hand down his well-muscled back and over the swell of his firm buttocks, enjoying his body and the fiery desire that it awoke within me. His hands explored my body as well, traveling down the curve of my hips, up the length of my thigh, until he reached my dripping slit.

"Oh, my sweet girl," he moaned into my neck.

"You are so wet," he moaned. He parted my folds with his fingers, seeking out my slick pearl. As he found it, I dug my nails into his back and moaned uncontrollably.

"Oh, Daddy!" I shivered as rubbed my button.

"That's right, sweet one. Let Daddy take care of this little pussy of yours," he said. He lowered himself, trailing kisses down my chest and stomach. He inhaled my scent deeply before his tongue traced the edges of my sopping pussy. As his tongue found my clit, I nearly screamed.

"Daddy, that feels so good!" He moaned against my slit as he bathed me with tender caresses. As he devoured me completely, I thrashed my head against the pillow and knew that I wouldn't last long against this onslaught of pleasure. He pressed a finger against my opening and plunged it in. His tongue was warm and gentle, and his finger was firm and persistent, and before long, orgasmic waves were building up, threatening to crash all over me. He continued nudging me toward sweet release until I could take it no more. I kicked my legs against the bed, ready to burst.

"Mmm, you taste so sweet. Cum for me, sweet girl," he moaned. His hot breath against my aching pussy felt like heaven. With one final burst of ecstasy, my climax overtook me. I shuddered and screamed, gripping Bill's hair and drenching his face. He sighed with satisfaction and grinned up at me as I collapsed against the covers, still twitching and moaning, the occasional aftershock washing over me. He wiped his face on the sheets before repositioning himself. He kissed me deeply; his tongue still heavy with my sweet juices.

"Good girl," he sighed, taking his rigid cock in his hand.

"Is this still ok, baby girl?" He said, slowing down and looking me in the eye. I bit my bottom lip and playfully thought for a moment before giggling and nodding. I like that I know I could have said no. It was my favorite thing about him that I knew I was safe with him. He rubbed his hard cock against my swollen clit, chuckling at how it made me jump before tracing it down my slick labia. I could feel his cock begin to press into me, stretching me open. I opened my legs wider, allowing him to plunge into me. He was so hard, and I was still very sensitive from my orgasm, and so I shuddered as he took me. He claimed me with his thick cock, affirming that I belonged to him. He grabbed my ass, holding me against him for a moment, savoring the sensation of being buried to the hilt inside of me, before thrusting into me again. Slowly, he parted me with his hardness, filling me up over and over.

"That's it, baby," he cried out.

"You're doing so good," he added. I moaned and grabbed his ass, pulling him deeper inside of me, craving more, craving everything he wanted to give to me. He felt better than anything I had ever experienced, seeming to know all the right spots to hit and, even better, made sure to hit them with every stroke.

"Oh, god! Fuck me!" I exclaimed. I didn't normally say such dirty things during sex but just then felt like a wild woman, and I wanted nothing more than to be his slut. His and his alone. My words seemed to drive him wild because he began to fuck me with abandon, as though he had finally unleashed the animal within. I ran my nails down his back and buttocks as he pounded into me, overwhelmed with pleasure. Over and over, his thrusts came faster and faster, his hands grabbed at my flesh, gripped my buttocks, my thighs, my hips.

His hands twisted into my hair, yanking my head back as he drove himself furiously into me, fast and hard.

"Is that what you wanted, princess? You like it when Daddy fucks you hard?" He groaned.

"Yes, Daddy. Yes! Yes!" I screamed. I was too lost in my pleasure to be articulate. Never before had I experienced such passion, such heat in a lover. I only wanted him to fuck me harder, faster, to never stop fucking me. His velvety voice was now ragged with lust as he growled and groaned with every penetration.

"Oh, my sweet baby. You're taking it like such a good girl. You feel so good around my cock. You are mine, mine, mine..." He groaned. He was so warm and hard inside of me, and I never wanted the night to end. I didn't have a care in the world, at that moment. All that mattered was that I was his and he was mine.

"You are so warm, my precious. So tight, so greedy for my cock," he said. At his deliciously sinful words, I clench tighter around him, causing him to shiver. I had never heard anyone talk like that before and it excited me. I could already feel another climax begin to build as his thick hard cock sent waves of intense pleasure throughout my entire being. My moans grew louder, and I thrashed my head from side to side, entirely overwhelmed by ecstasy. I tightened my thighs around him and held on as he guided me expertly to my second orgasm of the night. I let myself go completely, screaming and squirming underneath him as the most powerful orgasm I had ever had ripped its way through me.

As I quaked beneath him, I could feel him being pushed over the edge right along with me, his rhythm suddenly faltering as he cried out "baby girl!" and gripped my hair. I felt his warm seed coating my insides as he unleashed himself within me. He collapsed onto my breasts with a sigh, but I could still feel him pulsing inside of me. At last, the waves subsided, and we were left clinging to one another, breathless. He rested his forehead against mine, his arms wrapped tightly around me, still hard inside me. I felt utterly sated, content, and happy even. We lay like that for several minutes, catching our breath and exchanging tender kisses. Eventually, he rolled off me, lying flat on his back next to me, and pulled me to his chest. I let my fingers toy with his chest hair, not quite sure what to say.

"You've made quite the mess there, baby girl," he said, pointing to the large wet spot my multiple orgasms created.

"I think Daddy needs to give you a bath," he laughed.

Chapter 12

Bill held his hand under the faucet, checking the temperature of the running water before nodding that it was a safe temperature for his princess. He had filled the tub with bubbles and lit several scented candles, giving the small bathroom a dreamy, romantic atmosphere. Satisfied, he turned off the water and held out his hand for me.

"Ok, sweetheart. Let's get you clean. It's almost bedtime," he said. I took his hand and let him guide me into the tub. I lowered myself into the hot water, allowing the warmth to relax my muscles. I leaned back and closed my eyes happier than I had ever been at that moment.

"Feel good, little one?" Bill asked, his hand kneading the tense muscles of my neck.

"So good," I murmured. I slid further down into the hot water as he cupped his hands and began to wet my hair. The warm bubbles running down my scalp made me shiver with pleasure. As he began to work the shampoo in my hair, it felt amazing. His fingers were firm but sensual against my scalp. It felt so much sexier than when Nanny had done it for me all those times. I moaned and leaned my head back, not wanting him to miss a single inch. He grabbed a cup from the side of the tub and rinsed my hair until it was immaculate. He began to run a loofah over my body, slowly. He scrubbed my nipples, making me squirm a bit at the sensation, despite the thorough fucking I had just received. I sighed and arched my back, leaning into his strokes with the loofah.

"My baby girl is so greedy," he said playfully.

"Are you already feeling tingly again?" He asked. I giggled and nodded, feeling a bit shy suddenly. He moved his eyes up and down my body, obviously enjoying the sight. He moved the loofah down to my stomach, tickling me with its soft touch. I giggled but didn't pull away. He stroked my face lightly as he let the loofah trail lightly over my labia, making me squirm. Teasing me, he moved the loofah down to my feet, tickling the bottoms with a wicked grin. This time I can't help but jerk my foot back, squealing with laughter as water sloshed over the side.

"Oh, I think I've found the sweet spot!" he said with devilish delight. He moves menacingly toward my other foot, making me squeal "no," my giggles echoing off the bathroom tile.

"No? That's not the sweet spot? Hmm, I'd better keep searching then," he teased. He dropped the loofah and slid his fingers lightly over my soapy calves, stopping to tickle my knees.

"Is that the sweet spot?" He teased.

"Nope," I giggled.

"Are you sure?" He screwed his face up comically, feigning doubt.

"Keep going," I said, hiding my grin behind my hands. He shrugged and ran his hands up my thighs. At last, he finds my pussy under the warm water and lightly traces my folds before gently parting me. I melt at his touch and moan softly as his fingertip finds my clit.

"Oooh," he said.

"There it is. Is that better, pumpkin?" He questioned. I nod and bite my lip, my hand seeking out my breasts. I play with my nipples as he runs his finger slowly over my button, watching me writhe and fondle myself with wide-eyed fascination.

"Looks like we still need to work on using your words," he said firmly.

"I asked you if that feels better," he said slightly more sternly.

"That feels so much better, Daddy," I said breathlessly. His commanding tone and methodical stimulation were intoxicating.

"Good girl," he said, never taking his eyes off my hands as they continued to play with my tits. He was still naked, kneeling by the tub with a bath mat to cushion his knees. I noticed that his cock was already back at full-mast, and I longed to taste it.

"Daddy," I said squirming. I looked pointedly

at his erection, too shy to say it.

"What is it, baby girl?" He flicked my clit deviously, knowing that it would distract me further from being able to verbalize. He followed my line of sight, grabbing his massive erection with his free hand.

"Whatever could be the matter?" He asked, concern in his voice. I watched, mesmerized, as he slowly stroked his member while simultaneously stroking my pussy.

"I want … I want," I still couldn't get the words out. I had never asked for anything that I wanted before, sexually speaking. Usually, the guy just got himself off, and that was that. While I found the idea of saying those sexy words arousing, I couldn't quite get them out.

"What is it that you want, sweetheart?" He repositioned himself so that he brought that juicy cock closer.

"You can have anything you want. You have to ask," he gently said. I reached out to touch it, but he only swatted my hand away lightly before resuming his hypnotizing stroking.

"Come on, baby girl. Tell Daddy what you want," Bill lovingly said. I licked my lips and swallowed, screwing up my courage.

"Daddy, can I please s-suck your c-c-cock?" I stuttered a bit, but I managed to get it out. He sighed with pleasure at the sound of my words.

"Yes, baby girl. Of course, you can," he said, stroking my hair. He brought his cock to my lips, stroking my cheek lovingly. He pulled his hand from my pussy and replaced it with my own, leaving both of his hands-free to pet my hair as I took him gently into my mouth. At first, I only suckled the tip, savoring him. His cock still tasted of our combined flavors, and I moaned against his shaft. The slight vibration made him gasp softly.

"Good girl. You're doing so good," he said. He began to thrust in and out of my mouth slowly, testing my limits. I opened my mouth wider to take him deeper and twirled my finger around my slick pearl. As he thrusts deeper and deeper into my throat, I moan encouragingly, bobbing my head in the same rhythm. He threw his head back and moaned, resting his hand lightly on the back of my head, subtly encouraging me to take him even deeper. I worked his shaft down my throat until I felt myself gag lightly.

"That's it, kitten, choke on Daddy's cock," he said. I had never enjoyed deepthroating before, but something about the way he held my face tenderly contrasted with the dominant way he was inching his way down my throat made my pussy ache. I made a soft noise of pleasure as I rubbed my aching clit and tried to fit even more of him down my throat. I choked harder, and tears sprung to my eyes. He pulled back quickly, his face suddenly full of concern.

"Are you ok, sweetie? Did I hurt you?" He asked.

"I'm ok, Daddy. No, you didn't hurt me," I said. I opened my mouth to continue sucking him off, but he hesitates.

"We don't have to keep going if you don't want to," he said. I smiled up at him reassuringly.

"I want to," I said, reaching for his cock with my tongue.

"What did we say about asking for what we want?" His tone had shifted from concerned to playful, and he tapped his cock lightly against my tongue, giving me just a little taste.

"Please, may I choke on your cock some more Daddy?" I blushed deeply at my own words. I sounded so dirty! Daddy was thrilled to hear me talking dirty because he thrust into my mouth, filling my throat with his cock once more.

"Well, since you asked so nicely, little one," he grunted and pushed his cock as deep as it would go.

"Good girl, just a little deeper," he moaned. I choked and sputtered a little, drool dripping from my lips. As he pulled out slowly, more drool spilled out onto my chin and chest.

"Daddy's little drooly baby," he chuckled and

wiped my chin clean. I opened my mouth to receive him once more, but he shook his head.

"Stand up," he ordered. I obeyed him instantly, water cascading off of my naked body. He kissed me, pulling me close. The air was chilly on my wet skin, but his body was warm against mine, so I nestled closer against him, shivering. He grabbed a towel and wrapped it around me, helping me out of the bathtub. He dried me off, running the soft towel up and down my nude body, admiring every inch, and squeezed the water out of my hair with the terry cloth. Once dry, he stood back and took me in, his hand absentmindedly grabbing his cock as he drank me in with his eyes.

"Turn around," he commanded. I could practically feel his eyes burning into me as I stood there, silent and motionless, awaiting his next command.

"Walk to the counter," he commanded. I tiptoed across the tile, aware of both the slippery floor beneath my feet as well as how my backside might look to him, wanting it to look as perky as possible. I stop when I reach the counter and wait once more. He doesn't say anything for a moment, and I wonder if he is still stroking his cock, but I resist the temptation to look, know it will only earn me a spanking — nude, this time, with no thick diaper padding to protect me from his sharp blows.

"Bend over," he said, his voice getting thicker and lower from arousal. I put my hands on the sink for balance and bend at the hips, pointing my bottom in his direction. I hear him pad over on bare feet across the tile until he is standing directly behind me. Still, he watches me quietly. At last, I feel his hand on my bottom, running his hand over my silky smooth skin.

"You are so perfect, baby girl," he whispered. I feel his cock pressing between my ass cheeks, sliding slowly between them as he softly sighed. He kept sliding down until he found my slick opening, still wet and eager for him.

"Oh, you are Daddy's perfect slutty girl," he

said. He pressed his cock against my entrance but didn't enter me. I whimpered, burning with desire and yearning for him to take me again.

"What's wrong, princess?" he pressed his finger against my clit, sending a jolt of pleasure through me.

"Did you forget how to use your words again?" He questioned. I moaned and gritted my teeth, having grown slightly bashful once again. I strained towards his cock, but he stopped me with a firm, painful slap against my rear end. I jerked away from the pain, but he took me by the hips and pulled me against him once more.

"You are going to have to learn how to ask for my cock like a good little slut, is that understood?" He explained. To accentuate his point, he spanked me again, very hard. I winced and whimpered, unable to ignore how the pain made my pussy get even wetter. I pushed aside my embarrassment and found my words at last.

"I want you to fuck me," I said, blushing

deeply.

"I know you do, sweetheart. That's because you are Daddy's sweet little slut. Aren't you?" He asked. I nodded, but it wasn't good enough. *Smack.* Another jolt of pain and desire went through me as he slapped my bare ass.

"Tell me. Use your words," he growled.

"I'm Daddy's sweet little slut!" I cried out on the verge of tears. I was overwhelmed by pain, longing, and humiliation but far above all of that was the desperate desire to please him. He penetrated me but only slightly, not yet ready to give me my reward.

"That's right pumpkin. You are mine. Aren't you?" He asked.

"Yes, Daddy. I'm yours. I'm all yours. Please fuck me with your big hard cock. Please fuck me like a dirty little slut," I moaned as I felt him. The words came flooding out of me, begging him for sweet release. With one thrust, he finally gave me what I had been craving. He hammered into me, giving me the fucking I had begged for. His thick cock was hard as a rod inside of me, making me scream with every thrust. He put my hand on my pussy, guiding it to rub my clit as he pounded into me.

"Good little sluts cum when they are told to. Think you can do that, my princess? Think you can cum for Daddy?" He asked as I squealed with ecstasy as I rubbed my nub.

"Yes, Daddy. I can cum for you," I panted. I was already close; his cock and my finger combined had me building toward yet another climax.

"Not until I tell you to, ok, pumpkin?" He lovingly instructed.

"Ok, Daddy. I'll try it," I said. I hoped that I could wait, but his cock felt so good inside of me, I knew that it was going to be difficult. He dug his fingers into my hips, pulling me back to meet his every thrust.

"Oh, you're so tight, baby girl! So tight and so wet. Oh, you're going to make Daddy cum!" He groaned. I could feel him getting harder inside of me, his pace quickening. I knew I only had to hold on for a few moments longer.

"Cum for me!" he commanded at last. I moaned with sweet relief, letting my climax wash over me. Together we cried out, his hand finding mine on the counter as he pumped me full of cum for the second time that night.

"Good girl," he peppered the back of my neck with breathless kisses before gently withdrawing from me.

"You are such a good girl," he added, looking at my body. He toweled off my legs where our juices had coated my thighs before tossing the towel onto the floor to soak up the small puddle there. He lifted me and carried me back to his bed, lowering me gently onto the mattress. He curled up next to me, holding me close and burying his face in my hair. He caressed my body lovingly, letting his hands wander freely over my naked skin. Occasionally, he squeezed me tightly, making me squeal and giggle. Mostly, though, we just lied there in silence, enjoying the feeling of our naked bodies entwined with one another.

"Where's your pacifier?" he asked after a long time, a hint of sleepiness in his voice.

"In my duffle bag," I murmured, noticing that I was beginning to drift away as well.

"Wait here," he said, kissing my forehead and getting up. The bed felt big and cold without him, I noticed, so I got under the covers and waiting as he had instructed. I heard him in the bathroom, letting the water out of the tub and cleaning up the mess we had made. Then, I heard the clattering of dishes coming from the kitchen, and the refrigerator door open once or twice. Finally, he came back into the room carrying my pacifier and a fresh diaper for me. He leaned over me, gingerly placing the pacifier in my mouth and sealed it with a kiss.

"All ready for bed, little one?" He asked, already knowing the answer.

"Yes, Daddy," I said, the pacifier making my words lisp just a bit. He grinned and pinched my cheek lightly.

"Such a cutie. Ok, let's get your diaper on!" He said and pulled the covers back and had me scoot my bottom to the edge of the bed and put my legs up in the air. He took his time putting the diaper on me, savoring the process. Once on, he patted the front of it with a twinkle in his eye.

"You look so beautiful, princess," he said, reaching out and stroking my cheek affectionately. For the first time in my life, I felt beautiful. The way he looked at me like I was a precious jewel filled me with such pride. I was proud to be his. His baby girl.

"Would you like to stay in Daddy's room tonight, sweetheart?" He asked, my sleepy face lit up.

"Can I?" I gasped in happy bliss. He chuckled.

"Of course you can!" He exclaimed. He walked over to his closet and pulled out a teddy bear. I sat up and clapped my hands as he gave it to me.

"I've been saving this, waiting for someone

special to give it to. I've finally found her," he said. He kissed my forehead and then my pacifier again.

"My special girl," he said. Bill turned off the lights and joined me under the covers, pulling me close. I nestled my heavily padded bottom against him and closed my eyes, thoroughly content. I clutched my teddy bear close, feeling like the luckiest girl in the world.

"Goodnight baby girl," he whispered against my neck.

"Goodnight Daddy," I said, already drifting off to sleep.

Chapter 13

In the morning, I awoke to find that he was already up. I found a t-shirt in the closet and put it on. It was comically large, hanging almost to my knees, but it would serve for the moment. Groggily, I shuffled into the kitchen to find him making pancakes, as bright-eyed and bushy-tailed as if he had been awake for hours already.

"Good morning, sleepyhead," he chirped and kissing me on the forehead.

"Thought you were going to sleep all day," he playfully teased. He winked at me and patted the front of my diaper.

"Do you need changing?" He asked. He pulled the elastic out as he asked, visually checking my front to see that it was dry.

"No. I'm sorry, Daddy," I said and blushed.

"Well, that's no surprise. I made you squirt so

many times last night you didn't have anything left!" He laughed. Having expected to be chastised, I was caught somewhat off guard. He must have noticed my quizzical expression because he put down the spatula and pulled me close for a hug.

"You can wet your diaper, or not, anytime you choose, ok? If you feel like using the potty like a big girl, that's ok. If you'd rather have Daddy change you, that's ok too. Understood?" He said, looking me directly in my eye.

"Understood," I say, smiling. He patted my puffy rear.

"Good girl. Now, who's ready for some pancakes? I made yours with Mickey Mouse ears and chocolate chips for the eyes!" He exclaimed.

We chatted excitedly as we ate our breakfast and drank our coffee, planning what we would do that day. Bill suggested that after breakfast, we should relax on the couch and watch a little T.V for a while. Then, we could go for a walk and have a bit of lunch.

"And later, maybe we could go get you some

more permanent furniture for your room," he said as he blushed and suddenly seemed bashful.

"Or, for your apartment or whatever," he said quickly. I suppressed a laugh. He was so cute when he got like this, bashful and insecure. It was amazing to me how he could be so dominant and self-assured in the bedroom, yet act so nervous when it came to matters of the heart. As if he weren't completely perfect in every way.

"I think I'll be staying here for a while if that's ok with you?" He grinned at me, his shoulders dropping in relief.

"Yes! I was hoping that you would. I don't want to pressure you or make you feel trapped in any way. It's important to me that you are here because you want to be," he exclaimed, nodding enthusiastically.

"I want to be here," I said quickly, hoping that he would believe me.

"I want to be your baby girl more than anything," I said, eating my pancakes.

"I'm so happy to hear you say that," he said, kissing my forehead.

We cleaned up and set up camp on the couch. I have no idea what show he put on because we were so wrapped up in making out that I didn't pay it any attention. We never did make it out for that walk, either. This time when we made love, it was slow and sweet. He kissed me deeply as I rode him on the couch and afterward we cuddled, whispering and giggling together until cuddling turned to fucking once again. We enjoyed a simple lunch of sandwiches and sliced apples, deciding that we would try to find a chest of drawers for my room first so I would have somewhere to put all of my things.

"Not that I have many things," I said somewhat sadly.

"You will," he said, bucking up my chin.

"You can have anything you want. You know that," he said in a more serious voice than the one he usually used. We finally got dressed sometime after lunch. I was amused to see that his weekend attire was jeans and a t-shirt. I don't what I expected, exactly, I had just gotten so used to seeing him in tweed. I put on a t-shirt and a skirt. It seemed to amuse Daddy to reach under my diaper and squeeze my diaper.

We found a furniture store that would deliver. As we were about to go in, Bill realized that he had forgotten his wallet in the car.

"You go ahead, I'll catch up," he said, kissing me on the forehead and jogging back in the direction where we had parked. As I walked toward the entrance, I noticed a guy hanging around the cars. He was the kind of guy the old me would have been desperate to impress, saggy pants, stained tank top, drenched in cheap body spray. The sight of him brought back unpleasant memories of standing in parking lots just like this one, acting as a lookout for douchebags just like him as they tried to jimmy the locks of cars, looking for loose change and whatever they could steal from the gloveboxes.

"Hey little mama, how you doing?" he sneered at me suggestively as I walked by, quickening my pace. I would have been putty in this guy's hand last month. Now, I only wanted to get away from him, but he followed me.

"Hey, I'm talking to you," he said, raising his voice, angry at being ignored. I only waved vaguely in his direction and kept walking, hoping that he would leave me alone. His pace slowed, but he couldn't resist taking one last shot at me.

"You ugly anyway, you dumb bitch," he yelled. I heard a commotion behind me, and I turned around just in time to see Bill decking the guy in the face. The douchebag went down like a sack of potatoes, and Bill stood over him, his fist still clenched.

"Go get in the car, baby girl," he said, handing me the keys. I took them from him hurriedly and made a beeline for the car. I got behind the wheel in case we needed to make a hasty retreat and took deep breaths, trying to calm myself.

I set down a bowl of ice on the kitchen on the kitchen table and put Bill's hand into it. He had banged it up pretty badly on that guy's face, and he was starting to feel it. It had been a somewhat tense ride home, but he assured me that he was ok and that nothing was broken, only bruised. I just wasn't sure if it was the unpleasantness of what had just happened that made him so quiet or something else. I sat beside him and decided that if he wasn't going to talk then maybe I should.

"Thank you, by the way. You know, for defending my honor and all," I said. He chuckled at that, the first smile I had seen him crack in a couple of hours.

"I didn't scare you?" he asked.

"Is that what's been bothering you? No, sweetheart. You didn't scare me. You were my knight in shining armor," I replied. He was visibly relieved.

"I'm so glad. I don't normally act like that. I'm

not violent by nature. It's just when I heard him speaking to you like that and the way he was following you, I just, I lost it. Promise you weren't scared?" He asked again.

"He scared me. You were my hero. In fact," I got up and moved to his lap, wrapping my arms around his neck.

"It was more than a little sexy. The way you swooped in like some cowboy," I said. I kissed his nose, his forehead, his cheek. He sighed and wrapped his uninjured arm around me.

"Oh yeah?" He asked with a sideward smirk.

"Big time. No one has ever stood up for me before," I said nodding.

"You deserve it," he said, pulling my face down for a kiss.

"You deserve everything in the world. You're my baby girl, now, and no one will ever hurt you as long as I'm around. Understood?" He said.

"Understood," I repeated. He made me feel so safe and loved, more than I had ever thought possible. I was already longing for him again, despite the crazy amount of sex we'd had since I arrived yesterday afternoon.

Who knew happiness would be such an aphrodisiac? I thought as he pulled me down for another kiss, so full of heat and passion that I knew that he was feeling it too. He gripped my bottom, pulling me against his already hard cock.

"You drive me crazy, little one," he whispered, moaning as I ground my pussy against him.

"You are so sexy, so sweet," he continued covering my cheek in kisses. He trailed off and kissed my neck, brushing my hair back with the hand that just been in the ice, making me squeal and jump.

"Daddy, that's cold," I complained and poked my lip out. He laughed.

"Sorry! I forgot!" He laughed. I rubbed his injured hand between mine, bringing the blood back to it, and kissed the bruised spot.

"There, now it's all better!" I declared.

"That's right, pumpkin," he said, nuzzling my neck.

"You are the best nurse," he said. He licked my throat, nibbling and kissing me there until I was desperately squirming in his lap.

"What's wrong, sweetie?" he teased.

"You got ants in your pants or something?" He laughed.

"I've got the tingles," I admitted, putting his hand on the front of my diaper, showing him exactly where the offending tingles were.

"Oh, I guess we'll have to take care of that," he said. He put his hands under my bottom and lifted me onto the table. Sitting in the chair, he spread my legs open and reached under my skirt and pulled down my diaper.

"Show Daddy again where the tingles are," he said, looking at me expectantly. His eyes followed my every movement as I parted my folds for him to see.

"Hmm, yes I think I see the problem now. This pussy is dripping wet," he smirked.

"Oh, no!" I said, feeling both silly and horny, a new combination for me.

"What do we do?!" I giggled.

"You'll have to listen very carefully and do exactly what I say, ok, princess?" Bill said.

"Ok, Daddy! What should I do first?" I asked.

"First, I want you to touch your clit," he instructed. I put my finger on my button as he watched me closely.

"Good girl. Now move it around in a circle," he continued to instruct. I did as he said, twirling my finger and moaning softly as it sent ripples of excitement all through my body.

"Like that, Daddy?" I asked.

"Slower, baby girl. I don't want you to cum until I say so, ok?" He said. I slowed my pace as he had instructed. The slower pace amplified every sensation, making my entire body feel electric.

"I won't. I'll be a good girl," I moaned.

"I know you will. You're Daddy's good girl," he said. He watched with silent fascination as I fingered my pearl and moaned softly.

"Stop," he said suddenly. I took my finger off but whimpered and stuck out my lip. Daddy spanked the inside of my thigh.

"What's all that pouting, little one? If Daddy tells you to stop, you stop. Understood?" He said making me know that I better stop pouting.

"Yes, I understand," I said, trying not to show my disappointment on my face.

"Good girl. Now, put your finger inside that tight little pussy," he said. I sank my finger into my eager hole, my thigh still stinging. Eagerly, I sought out the sweet spot under his watchful eye, sighing with pleasure once I found it.

"Does that feel good, pumpkin?" He asked, already knowing the answer.

"Yes, Daddy. That feels so good," I replied. His eyes twinkled.

"Good. Now, move it in and out. Remember to go slow," he said. I loved having his gaze upon me as I pleasured myself. I went as slow as I could, moving my finger in and out of my aching pussy, noticing how it ached all the more for the hungry look he was giving me. He looked ready to devour me, but he only watched.

"Now, use two fingers," he said, continuing to tease me with his slow instructions. I swallowed, never having put two in before. *Smack*. My hesitation cost me as he brought his hand down on my other thigh, leaving behind a red mark.

"What did I say about doing what Daddy tell you?" He commanded.

"I'm sorry, Daddy," I said, biting my bottom lip, not wanting to disappoint him.

"Don't be sorry. Just do what I tell you," he replied. I nod and put a second finger inside, inching it in slowly. I feel myself stretch open to accommodate it and it feels so deliciously good that I let my head roll back and moan.

"See pumpkin? Daddy knows what's best for you and that slutty little pussy of yours. Isn't that right?" He questioned.

"Yes, Daddy knows best," I said, my fingers buried in my slick canal. Another whack on my thigh and Daddy's voice turned authoritative.

"Am I going to have to get my belt? Daddy knows best about what?" He asked. His control over me was intoxicatingly erotic.

"What's good for me and my slutty little pussy," I gasp. The stinging pain that lingered on my thigh heightened the pleasure I was giving myself.

"Daddy?" I ask, my voice taking on a high pitched, pleading quality.

"Yes, pumpkin?" He said, running his hands over my thighs. He never took his eyes off my fingers as the disappeared and reappeared from my dripping pussy.

"Can I cum? I need to cum. Pretty please?" I begged. I hoped that if I asked very nicely, he would grant my request, maybe even fuck me and let me cum on his big yummy cock.

"You are a perfect girl for asking first. But no," he said, making me almost whimper.

I tried very hard not to pout, knowing it would only earn me another spanking on my thigh. He stood from his chair and pulled his cock out.

"Daddy gets to go first, tonight," he said. He started stroking his cock, continuing to watch me finger my pussy. It was so tantalizing, seeing his cock so close but not being allowed to touch it, only being allowed to fuck myself slowly. I ached to feel his throbbing hardness inside, pounding me closer and closer to the edge.

"Stop," he barked, and I quickly pulled my fingers out, panting with desire. He smiled, stroking his cock faster.

"Good girl. You're such a good little slut for Daddy, aren't you?" He asked.

"Yes, I'm a good little slut for Daddy," I said. I blush as I say the words and my pussy begs for stimulation. I loved being dirty for him, how it only brought us closer together. It feels so good knowing that he isn't here for a quick fuck. No, he will settle for nothing less than owning me completely and ruining me for all other men.

"Pull your lips apart. Let me see my beautiful girl," he said. I spread my legs open wide and part my hairless pussy for him to see. I'm so wet that I glisten under the kitchen light.

"Oh, baby, you're so beautiful," he said, almost mesmerized by my body. I blush again. Never before has someone looked at me so intimately and with such raw passion. He strokes his cock furiously, his eyes glued to my pussy splayed out before him.

"I'm going to cum," he announced, positioning his cock over my pussy.

"Keeps those lips open, baby girl. My sweet, dirty girl," he groaned. With a loud grunt, he lets himself go, spraying my pussy, tummy, and tits with his cum. It felt so warm and gooey as it hit my flesh, and I felt as though he is marking me. The idea set my whole body on fire, loving how it felt to be his. He pushed his still hard cock into me, making my eyes roll back in my head.

"Do you want to cum on Daddy's cock?" he

asked, putting my hand on my clit as he thrust into me.

"Yes! Can I please cum on your cock, Daddy?" I begged.

"Yes, baby girl," he said. He pumped into me, hard and fast, already familiar with the pace that drives me the wildest.

"Go ahead and make yourself cum," he said. I rubbed my clit, still slick with his jizz, as he split me open. Seconds later, my whole body was on fire as the climax came on me hard and fast. I quaked and screamed, totally lost in the ecstasy. I soaked him and the kitchen floor as I was taken by wave after wave. Finally, I was spent, and he chuckled approvingly.

"That was a big one!" He exclaimed. He scooped me up and took me to the bathroom to get cleaned up. Wetting a washcloth, he tenderly wiped me down, cleaning all the sweat and jizz off of me. Once I was all clean and dry, he picked me back up and carried me to the bedroom.

"You've had a long, hard day," he said as he lay me down on the covers.

"I think it's time for a nap," he added.

"That sounds nice," I agreed as he snuggled up next to me.

"Know any good lullabies?" I said, cuddling his arm.

"Just one," he whispered and began humming gently in my ear. The soothing sound worked like a charm, and I drifted off in his arms.

Chapter 14

Bill had some jello waiting for me when I woke up.

"Sex, sleep, and snacks? You certainly know how to keep a woman happy, don't you?" I tease, joining him on the couch.

"I hope so. That's the plan anyway," he said. He paused the video game he had been playing and wrapped his arm around my waist and pulled me close. I laid my head against his shoulder, wiping the sleep from my eyes.

"How are you feeling? I hope that jerk didn't upset you too much," he said, holding my face in his hands and looking me in the eye.

"I feel fine, honestly. Let's forget about him," I said.

"Good," he smiled.

"But, while we're on the subject of feelings, I want you to know that I've spoken with my colleague

Dr. Saperstein and he is going to be taking over your therapy," he said. I pulled back a little, startled.

"You think I need therapy?" I gasped, a frown forming on my forehead.

"I think everyone needs therapy, said the therapist," he laughed.

"Seriously, though. We ended your treatment at the Institute early, and I want to make sure that it doesn't cause any unforeseen problems. A Daddy has to make sure his baby girl is completely healthy," he tapped my forehead lightly.

"Including up here," he said.

"Does he do age regression therapy like you do?" I smiled and conceded.

"No, but he is familiar with it. He is also familiar with age-play as a lifestyle so you can tell him anything and you don't have to be embarrassed," he said. I nodded, feeling better about the whole thing already.

"And seriously," he continued, cupping my face with his hands.

"Don't feel weird about being in therapy. Everybody has stuff they have to work out," he said before he kissed me softly, then pressed the jello snack into my hand.

"Now be a good girl and eat your snack," he said.

"Ok, Daddy. Will you help me with the top?" I asked. He pulled the silver foil off the top, and I dug in my spoon.

"Thank you for taking such good care of me, Daddy," I said around a mouthful of orange jello.

"I'll always take care of you, baby girl," he said.

The rest of the weekend went well. We decided to shop online for furniture, not wanting to leave our little love nest. Daddy told me to pick out anything I wanted and not to worry about the price.

I spent all of Sunday afternoon in my little space. Daddy watched me color, play with my stuffies, and even read to me when it was nap time. I drew him funny pictures of him and Nanny which he put on the fridge, affixed with colorful magnets. He let me help him make dinner, explaining to me patiently all the steps, and why it was essential to follow each one, watching with pride as I tried to follow his instructions. I felt so relaxed in my little space, forgetting all about my grownup worries. I wish I had known about being a little earlier. It would have been a beautiful escape. When Sunday night rolled around, I found myself getting nervous about Daddy going to work Monday morning and leaving me at home all alone. At first, I didn't say anything, hoping that it would pass, but as we were getting ready for bed, he asked me about it directly.

"Do you think you'll be alright while I'm at work tomorrow, sweetheart?" I fidgeted nervously and looked at the floor, embarrassed by my anxiety.

"I don't know," I replied. He put down the pillow he had been fluffing and rushed over to put his arms around me. He cupped my face with my hands and forced my face up to look at him.

"What's wrong little one? No, don't look away. What's bothering you?" He asked.

"I'm not sure, exactly. Just when I think about being here all alone tomorrow, I get a tight feeling in my chest," I said.

"Ok," he said slowly.

"Do you want me to call Dr. Saperstein and see if he can fit you in tomorrow," he said.

"No," I replied quickly.

"I don't want to make a bit deal about it. It will only make it worse," I said.

"Well, we don't want that," he said.

"Ok, how about this. You can text me anytime you want tomorrow. I won't always be able to write you back right away. I have patients to see. But you can write to me as often as you like and I promise to read them as soon as I can," he said. I thought about that, and it did sound a little better, knowing that I could contact him at any time.

"And," he said, pulling my teddy bear out from under the bed where it had fallen.

"Hamilton will be here to keep you company," he added.

"Oh, is that his name?" I asked.

"Sure, didn't he tell you?" He asked before he addressed Hamilton directly.

"How rude of you, not introducing yourself," he said. I giggled, wondering how I had gotten so incredibly lucky to have found such a sweet and sexy man.

"Well," he continued chastising the bear.

"You had better be a lot more friendly to Molly tomorrow, Mr. Hamilton or you'll have me to answer to when I get home," he said. He handed the bear back to me and put his hands over its ears whispering.

"I'm so sorry he's not normally like that," he playfully said.

"You're so silly, Daddy!" I exclaimed.

"I sure am," he said as he pulled me close once more and kissed me lightly on the lips.

"Feeling a little bit braver about tomorrow?"

He asked as he tucked me into bed.

"Yes, Daddy. I'll be brave," I replied as I fell asleep.

I did well the first part of the day. Daddy made breakfast, just as he had all weekend. I watched him get dressed and sent him off to work with a kiss. T.V kept me distracted for the better part of the morning. Daddy texted once or twice to check-in, and I reported that everything was good so far. I made myself some lunch and cleaned up a little. Bill was pretty neat for a bachelor, however, so that didn't keep me very occupied for very long. The afternoon is when things got bad. Afternoons had always been hard for me. I get tired and cranky. I knew that I should try to take a nap, but I was too restless. I tried cuddling with my teddy bear, but it did not soothe me enough to drift off to sleep. I tried texting Daddy, but he was with a patient and didn't write me back. Eventually, I just sank onto the kitchen floor and cried, trying to figure out why I felt this way.

***

Bill was having a hard time concentrating on his staff meeting with Nurse Roberts. He knew Molly was having a difficult time at home, and it killed him that he couldn't be there for her. His phone vibrated on the desk repeatedly.

"Do you need to get that?" Deborah asked after the eighth text in a row.

"It's Molly," Bill said, picking up the phone.

"She's having a difficult time adjusting," he said.

"Poor dear," said Deborah. They had gotten close during Molly's time at the Institute. Bill's wasn't the only heart his baby girl had captured.

"I can't decide if I should take a personal day to be with her. I hate seeing her upset, but on the other hand, maybe she needs to learn a little more independence. What do you think I should do,

Deborah?" He asked, feeling slightly lost.

"I think you should stay here and let me go check in on the poor girl," she replied, hoping he would agree, smiling when he nodded.

"Yes, that's the perfect compromise, I think. She shouldn't have to go through this alone. I'll text her and ask if she's up for company," he said. He had barely put the phone back down when he got his reply, and he chuckled as he read it.

"She says yes with fourteen exclamation marks. I'd say she's up for it," Bill said.

Chapter 15

I danced around the living room excitedly, eager to see Nanny again. It had only been a couple of days since I had seen her last but so much had happened since then. After what felt like hours but was probably only forty-five minutes, her car pulled into the driveway. I met her on the porch, and we hugged. I showed her around the house, proud of the small little changes I had already made to make the place feel a little less like a bachelor pad and a bit more like home. I poured us both a cup of coffee, and we sat at the small kitchen table to chat. She told me more about her life, and I learned that she had three grandkids that lived far away. Her husband had passed away many years back, and my heart ached for her, knowing all too well what it was like to lose someone much too soon.

"So, my dear," she said, bringing the

conversation around to me.

"Bill tells me you're having a bit of a day," she said.

"I've had worse, I guess. I'm just not used to being alone. I've always had to share a space. I know that having a big house all to myself is a luxury, it's a luxury I've dreamed of all my life, but now that I have it, it's a lot to get used to. I don't know what to do with myself all day," I said, shrugging my shoulders. She nodded and took a sip of her hot drink, considering.

"Do you think you'll want to get a job?" She said, making me sighed.

"That kind of freaks me out, too. I've never been able to keep a job for very long. Always getting in fights with the customers," I honestly replied.

"Well, maybe not right now then. Sounds to me like you need a hobby. What do you like to do for fun?" She replied.

"I don't know. I've always just done whatever my friends wanted to do," I replied.

"Well, I think it's time to figure out what Molly wants to do. Why don't you spend this week trying out different activities? Maybe you could take a few different classes a week until something feels right," I said.

"That's an excellent idea, Nanny!" I exclaim.

"But do you think Da - I mean Bill will pay for it? I don't have any money, you know," I said, a bit embarrassed. Nanny laughed, a deep belly laugh as though I had hit on comedy gold.

"Child, that man would give you anything and everything you could ever ask for, haven't you figured that out by now?" She questioned, making me blush.

"I know. I still get nervous asking for things sometimes," I replied. She nodded sympathetically.

"It will come with time. Just keep working at it. Remember, everything is a process," she said reassuringly. She downed the last of her coffee in one big gulp and stood to go.

"It was really lovely to see you again, my

dear. I hope we do this again sometime soon," she said. We hugged, and she returned to work.

I spent the rest of the afternoon looking up pottery classes, yoga classes. You name it. Poor Daddy was going to have a whole list of activities to help me with when he got home. I giggled, thinking of how he would probably be delighted. Nanny was right, as always. Bill would help me in any way he could. I was so engrossed in what I was doing that I didn't even notice that it was almost time for Daddy to get home until he texted me.

Nanny says that you're feeling better. How was the rest of your afternoon? His message read.

Good. I am feeling better. I replied, smiling as I typed.

I have to stop by the store. I'll be home soon. XOXO. Came his last reply. I decided to put on a little makeup and a nice shirt, wanting to look nice when he came home. Just as I was putting on the finishing touches, I got another text.

I want you naked and kneeling by the front

door in ten minutes. I felt a thrill go through me. Daddy had the best games. I stripped myself down and waited, already wet with excitement as I imagined the possibilities. When he came home, he had shopping bags in his hands. He noticed me, kneeling as per his instructions and smiled.

"Good girl," he said softly. He put down the bags and began slowly taking off his jacket and tie, watching my naked form as he did so. I stayed still, letting him claim me with his eyes, waiting for his next set of instructions.

"I missed you today, baby girl," he said as his shirt came off. He let his clothing fall carelessly to the floor.

"I missed you too, Daddy," I said, enjoying the view as he began taking his pants off.

"I'm glad you're home," I said.

"Me too, pumpkin," he replied. The boxers came off, and he stood before me in all his naked glory, his toned body moving as gracefully as a cat as he closed the small space between us.

"Open wide," he said, grasping his stiff cock. Eagerly, I opened my mouth, moaning at the taste of him as he slid his erection on my soft, wet tongue. "I've been thinking about this sweet little mouth all day," he explained. He grabbed the back of my head and eased his cock further down my throat. I looked up at him as he penetrated my mouth, dripping wet as I enjoyed the look of ecstasy on his chiseled face, knowing how much pleasure I was bringing him. He stroked my face as I choke on him, whispering encouragement as he gently pushed my limits.

"Keep that mouth open," he said as he pulled out. Drool dribbled down my chin and chest. He smiles down at, enjoying the sight.

"Did you like that, baby girl?" I nod, my mouth still open. He placed the head of his cock on my tongue.

"Do you want some more?" He asked, looking into my eyes.

"Uh-huh," I said. I nod again, my tongue caressing the sensitive underside of his cock. He pushed in, still testing my limits. I moaned as he slid down my throat. As his meaty erection cuts off my air supply, I notice how it intensifies every sensation. He began to pull back, but I grab his hips, reflexively pulling his back. He watches, fascinated, as I struggled to keep him down, not wanting to let go just yet. Who knew that I loved deepthroating so much?

I love deepthroating Daddy. Not just anyone. Only Daddy, I thought. He pulled out as I was beginning to get light-headed. He stroked his cock, watching me gasp for air.

"Are you ok, baby girl?" He asked, checking in to make sure that I still felt safe and comfortable. I nodded and swallowed.

"Yes, Daddy. I love sucking your cock," I said. I was glowing with pride as to how well I was using my words, not to mention what good slut I was for him. He looked at me with tenderness and heat in his eyes.

"Good girl," he purred.

"You're so sexy, little one. I love watching you suck me off. Ready for some more?" He asked, love, pouring from his eyes.

"Yes, please," I squeal and open my mouth wide. He sinks his cock in, even deeper than before. I relax into it, wanting to swallow him completely. In my eagerness, I go a little too far and choke, tears springing to my eyes.

"Go slow, baby girl. We'll get there," he reminded me. He set a hypnotizing pace, fucking my throat slowly but steadily. Even as his lust built, he still checked in with me regularly and caressed my face lovingly, telling me what a good girl I was. The more he praised me, the more my pussy tingled and dripped with desire. I kept my hands at my sides, however, knowing that he wouldn't like it if I touched myself without his permission. I swallowed his cock over and over, hoping that he would allow me to cum soon.

"Oh, baby, you're going to make Daddy cum. Do you want to swallow it?" Bill asked. The thought sent a thrill through me.

"Yes, Daddy. Please give me your cum. I want to swallow it all," I reply, trying to open my throat even more for him. My lips brushed against his cock as I spoke, and the sound of my sexy words made him go over the edge. I felt his cock pulse and opened my mouth eagerly. He shouted as he pumped my mouth full and I swallowed every bit of it down.

"Oh, baby," he said, coming back down to earth.

"You're such a good girl. I'm so proud of you," he said. He bent down and kissed me softly on the forehead.

"Daddy got you some new toys today, do you want to see?" He said, smiling at me. I nodded eagerly. My pussy was in dire need of attention, but it was hard not to get excited about new toys.

"Yes, gimme gimme," I squealed, and he laughed, bringing the shopping bags over to where I was still kneeling.

"Open this one first," he said, handing me one of the bags. I tore past the tissue paper to find a butt plug and some lube at the bottom. It was a pretty thing, something I didn't even know was possible, shiny silver with a sparkly pink jewel at the end. I picked it up to look at it and saw that it had "Daddy's girl" etched onto it. I blushed, not sure what to say. I had never used one of those before.

"Ok, now this one," he said, handing me the other bag. Inside I saw a vibrator. The box bragged about the many settings and attachments it offered. I blushed harder, wondering if Daddy was going to use this on me. My pussy was still aching, and I was desperate for relief.

"What do you think? Want to try them?" I felt a bit shy, never having used any props before, but I was also curious.

"Ok Daddy, let's try them," I said, biting my bottom lip.

"If you don't like them, you have to tell me. No lying," he said looking at me dead in the eye. His voice was firm, and my insides clenched, responding to his dominance.

"I promise, Daddy. No lying," I reply, my eyes going wide.

"Good girl," he said. He took the butt plug and lube from the bag.

"Bend over," he ordered, and I got onto all fours. I heard him opening the lube and waited, unsure what to expect. I felt it press against my rear entrance, cold and slippery.

"How's that?" he asked.

"Okay so far," I said, holding my breath.

"Good. I'm going to push it in more. Let me know if I need to slow down," he instructed. He slid it in slowly. It wasn't very big and, to my surprise, it fit very easily inside of me. It felt nice once he worked it in. I had never been stimulated there before, and it made my pussy tingle. He stepped back to admire his handiwork.

"Oh, princess, you look so pretty. And you're sure it feels ok?" Bill asked.

"Yes, Daddy. I like it," I said. I could feel my heart racing with excitement.

"I'm glad. You can wear this anytime you like, okay pumpkin?" His fingers searched out my pussy, running along my labia and barely grazing my clit, causing me to twitch.

"Oh sweetie, you're so wet. Let's get you taken care of. Stay right there," he said. I remain on all fours as I listened to him take out the vibrator. He turned it on the lowest setting and pressed it against my pussy, causing me to moan and lean into it. It was the most delicious sensation I've ever experienced, sending waves of unspeakable pleasure all over my body.

"I think my baby likes that one," he chuckled, turning the vibrator off again. I moaned and yearned my hips backward, seeking the stimulation that was now gone.

"In a minute, sweetie. Let's you comfortable. Crawl to our bedroom. I wanna see that little tushie wiggle all down the hallway," he said, the smile on his face telling me all I needed to know. I started moving slowly, feeling somewhat drunk on desire. With every movement, I was made aware of the buttplug still inside of me, teasing me with its subtle sensations. I was also acutely aware of his eyes on my backside, loving the way he loved to look at me and how sexy it always made me feel.

Chapter 16

When I reached the bedroom, he picked me up and placed me on the bed face up.

"Daddy's in charge," he reminded me, spreading my legs.

"You are not allowed to touch yourself until I say so, understood," he added.

"I'll try, Daddy," I said, knowing how much of a challenge that will be.

"If you don't think you can resist, say so, and Daddy will tie your hands together for you. I know how horny my baby gets," he chuckled. I considered it for a moment and realized that he is right. I was so turned on. I would never be able to resist.

"You'd better tie me up," I said, eager to try yet another new fun game. He grabbed one of his ties and wrapped it around my wrists firmly; however, not so tight that it hurt my wrists.

"There. Now lie back and let Daddy take over now," he said. I sighed happily as he turned the vibrator back on. Letting Daddy take charge felt so good and so right. I relaxed my legs open as he touched the vibrator to my clit. Again, my body was filled with the most delicious sensations, and I writhed on the bed. He had just begun, and already I was close to orgasming. My hands were restrained above my head, so I could only squirm and moan, entirely at his mercy.

"Oh, Daddy. I need - I need to cum. Please, can I cum?" I begged.

"Go ahead, kitten," he said. As soon as he said the words, my orgasm came gushing out of me. I screamed and quaked, the steady vibration sending powerful waves of pure ecstasy. The waves receded, but Daddy did not pull the vibrator away. He kept it right where it was, a devious twinkle in his eye.

"Daddy," I said, squirming away as I grew more sensitive.

"What are you doing?" I added.

"I told you, little one. Daddy is in charge now. Stop squirming, or you'll get a spanking," he said. I settled back down or tried to anyway. I moaned and whined and squealed, the pleasure going between too much of a good thing and not enough. He began to manipulate my butt plug, sliding it in and out as I sputtered and squirmed. This time, however, I wasn't squirming away. The anal stimulation was sending me towards another climax, and I squirmed against the vibrator.

"Such a greedy baby. Are you already ready to cum again, sweet girl?" He said.

"Can I Daddy?" I begged, breathless, and horny.

"You can cum as many times as you like while Daddy is in charge, sweet one. I want to see just how many times I can make you squirt," he said. He bent over and nibbled my nippled, still manipulating my butt plug and I came again, even harder than the first time.

"Daddyyyy!" I cried out, thrashing my head

from side to side as I let go. My breathing began to calm once more, but he still held the vibrator against my swollen clit. I kicked my legs and squealed.

"Oh, Daddy. I don't think I can anymore," I whined.

"You'd better try, pumpkin. Daddy isn't done with you yet," he said. I felt his hard cock press against my entrance, filling my sensitive pussy, making me scream with every inch. I was beyond all words, and all thought. He was in control, and I was his puppet. He thrust into me hard and fast, torturing me with pleasure from his cock, and the vibrator still pressed against my clit. I lost track of how many times I peaked. It seemed to go on forever. Finally, I felt his testicles tighten against me and heard him cry out my name. We climaxed together before collapsing into a sweaty, sticky pile. Movement seemed impossible for a very long time. I had turned entirely to jello. Finally, he disentangled himself from me and instructed me to stay where I was.

No problem there, I thought with a snicker.

He returned with a sippy cup full of water and told me to drink every last job.

"Can't have my baby girl getting dehydrated," he said softly, taking the plastic cup from me and putting it on the bedside table. We cuddled and chatted. I told him about Nanny's suggestion and the classes I had found online. He was very excited about the idea and even wanted to take a couple of them with me. Our tummies began to rumble, so we finally emerged from the bedroom like two bears waking up from winter hibernation on the hunt for food.

Chapter 17

We found our clothes and got dressed, conceding that it was probably a bad idea to cook naked. I left my plug in, however, loving how it secretly marked me as his. He poured me a big glass of juice while he cooked and I chatted happily away, excited about my new classes. After we ate, he helped me get everything booked, once again telling me to not worry about the cost.

"I told you you could have anything you want and I meant it. I'm no millionaire, but I can take care of my baby girl. We'll have to schedule your classes around my work hours for now, but we should get you a nice, safe, reliable car pretty soon. Then, you can come and go as you please," he explained. He also suggested that a bit more structure in my life might help with my adjustment.

"What do you mean?" I asked. "Structure"

was one of those words that teachers and guidance counselors liked to use but never took the time to explain.

"I think I should make a schedule for you, so you don't feel so lost all day. You mentioned that you didn't know what to do with yourself all day. This way, you'll know exactly what to do and at what time to do it," he said.

"So, you want to make a list of chores for me?" I whined. I scrunched up my nose, not exactly loving the thought. Then again, I supposed it was only fair, seeing as he was letting me live here rent-free. I should do something to give back.

"Chores might be a part of it, sure. But it will also be things like going to your classes and scheduled snack time and nap time. What do you think?" he asked.

"Let's try it!" I said. There was something about him taking control that completely, even of my mundane, everyday tasks, sent a thrill of arousal through me. I bit my lip as I watched him draw up a schedule, planning out my activities for the week. It was arousing, yes, but it also made me feel so safe and so loved, knowing that he cared about every detail of my life this intensely. No had ever shown me this much attention or affection, not since my parents died. Sometimes, I would wish that I could remember them better, but I was also incredibly grateful to have Bill. He made me feel like I finally had someone I could rely on.

"What do you think of that, pumpkin?" He handed the schedule to me, but I hardly looked at it. My trust in him was so complete that I glanced it over briefly and declared that it looked very nice indeed.

"Good. Try it out for a few days, and we'll see if we need to make any adjustments," he said. I got up to take care of the dishes, but he took the plate from my hand before I could even get it to the sink.

"Why don't you let Daddy take care of that while you put some fresh sheets on the bed?" He asked.

"What's wrong, don't trust me with sharp objects?" I teased. He laughed.

"I would trust you with anything, baby girl. You're the smartest and the bravest girl I know. It's just that Daddy likes to be in control, and that includes in the kitchen. If the dishes aren't loaded in just the right way well, it bothers me, that's all," he explained. I nodded.

"I get that. I get particular about my sticker collection sometimes," I said understandably.

After we had gotten our chores done, Daddy gave me a bubble bath, thoroughly sudsing me up from head to toe. As he ran the loofah over my pussy, I could feel myself reacting to his touch. Even after the countless climaxes, he had given me earlier. I was still so greedy for him. I could never get enough of how sexy and pampered he made me feel. The dominant energy came off of him in waves, and I always found it incredibly intoxicating.

"Looks like it's time for shaving, little one," he

said. I instinctively grabbed for the razor, but he took it from me.

"Daddy is going to take care of that from now on, understood?" He said. He lathered my legs with shaving cream and ran the hard metal over my flesh, lightly and slowly. As he shaved me, his face took on that hungry look, and my fire for him grew even hotter.

This man is going to be the death of me, I thought happily, twisting so that he could shave all of my hard to reach places. The tub was too small for him to effectively shave my pussy, however, so he rinsed and dried me off and laid a towel down on the bathroom floor for me to lie on. He warmed the shaving cream between his hands before spreading it out over my mound and labia, letting his fingers linger over my clit. The foamy bubbles tingled and tickled the short hairs that had grown back in over the past few days, and I squirmed a little. He held the razor gently against my mound.

"Stay still, pumpkin. Daddy will have you

taken care of in no time," he said. I held my legs open as he shaved me. The intense way he was staring at me and the way his breath started to come faster as he ran the sharp metal over my sensitive skin made it a much more erotic experience than when Nanny had done it for me. As he spread my lips to make sure he had done a thorough job, I heard him suck in air appreciatively at what he found.

"Oh sweetie, do you like when Daddy shaves your pussy? Just look at how wet you've gotten," he said. He wiped the remaining shaving cream off with a wet cloth and went right back to inspecting my pussy carefully. The hungry way he looked at my pussy was so tantalizing to watch.

"Yes," I moaned as he touched me.

"I love it when you shave me, Daddy," I said. My labia felt so bare and exposed, and every stroke of his fingers set my body on fire. I was slick with desire, even after the bath. I wondered if I would ever be not horny around him and hoped that I wouldn't. He moved his finger slowly, watching every twitch and moan with intense scrutiny.

"Do you want Daddy to make you cum again?" his voice was so velvety smooth and sexy. His face was hovering just above my clit, and I could feel his hot breath wash over me. All he would have to do is reach out his tongue just a little.

"Yes, Daddy. Please lick my slutty pussy and let me cum all over your tongue," I moan. I was getting better at the dirty talk, but I probably would always blush just a little when I said such filthy things, as much as they made my pussy ache. Suddenly, he stopped. He pulled back and lifted me off the ground. I wrapped my legs around him eagerly, but he only put me back down onto my feet.

"No, that's enough for tonight, little one. It's bedtime now," I whimpered and pouted. My pussy felt like it was on fire. How could he do that to me, get me all hot and bothered and then leave me hanging?

"That was mean, Daddy!" I said, poking my lip out even further.

"You'd better wipe that pout off that cute little face, baby girl. Daddy says no more, and that's how it's going to be," he ordered. He led me back into the bedroom.

"Do you want Daddy to put a diaper on you tonight or are you feeling like a big girl," he said. I was still upset, however. Being shaved by him had aroused me greatly, and I didn't like being denied release. I refused to answer him. Instead, I crossed my arms and pouted. His expression immediately grew stern.

"No, baby," he said firmly.

"What did I say about that pout. You have to learn that Daddy is in charge," he said. Again, I didn't answer him not verbally anyway. I scrunched up my face and stuck my tongue out at him. He sighed.

"Ok, baby girl, you asked for it," he said, shaking his head. He pulled my still-naked form over his knee and brought his hand down on my bottom. It hurt so much more than it had when I had my diaper on, even more than the playful smacks he had given me during our lovemaking. I jerked with every blow, tears springing to my eyes, and I try to wriggle my way off of his lap. I don't get far before he grabs my waist and pulls me back, spanking me even harder.

"Daddy, please! I'm sorry, I won't pout anymore," I cried.

"I know you're sorry," he said calmly, continuing to smack my bottom.

"But you have to learn your lesson. You have to learn that Daddy is in charge," he growled. I try to reach back to block the blows but quickly pinned my hands down with one hand while continuing to spank me with the other. I sobbed, and I kicked, but nothing I did made him stop. He didn't stop until my bottom was bright red, feeling like it was on fire. At last, he relented, rubbing my inflamed flesh lightly.

"Are you going to behave now?" he asked softly, his hand stroking my back and thighs as well.

"Yes, Daddy," I sniffled. He lay back on the bed, pulling me on top of him. My still damp hair fanned out around us as I nestled into his broad chest, wiping the tears from my eyes. The spanking had done nothing to quell my desire if anything the pain in my bottom only made me want him more, but I was determined to be a good girl for him.

"You took your spanking like a good girl, Daddy's proud of you," he whispered and rubbed my back. As he ran his hands over the tender flesh of my bottom, I winced.

"It hurts," I whined. Daddy chuckled and rolled me onto my back.

"It's supposed to hurt, sweetheart. That's what makes it a punishment. Now, every time you sit down over the next few days, you'll remember who you belong to," he said.

"I belong to you, Daddy," I said without hesitation, wrapping my arms sleepily around his neck.

"You sure do, baby girl," he murmured against my neck. I could tell that he was getting sleepy as well.

"You always will. I'm going to take care of you. I'll never let anything bad ever happen to you again," he said. We fell asleep like that, wrapped tightly in one another's arms.

Chapter 18

I awoke to feel something brush between my legs. I looked over to Daddy's pillow to see that he wasn't there. Then, I felt his tongue brush up against my clit. I moaned and opened my legs, eager to allow him more access.

"You're still wet from last night," he noted with satisfaction.

"You must need it bad," he added.

"Yes, Daddy. I do need it bad. I need YOU bad," I beg. I ran my fingers through his silky brown hair as he gave my pussy a long, slow lick, twirling his tongue around my swollen clit. He lapped at me, making my legs quiver. I threw my head back against the pillow and moaned.

"That's it, pumpkin," he said, sliding a finger into me.

"Show Daddy how much you like it. Play with

your breasts," he said.

He resumed his attention to my clit but watched to make sure that I obeyed. I grabbed my breast and pinched my nipples as he watched in the dim predawn light. He slid his hands under my butt. My flesh was still bruised and sore, and it stung as he dug in his fingers, bringing my hips closer to his face. The combined sensations of pleasure and pain drew me closer to orgasm, and I squirmed against Daddy's mouth not sure if he would allow it. I whined and kicked my legs, trying to work up the courage to ask. Just then he stopped and repositioned himself on top of me. He kissed me deeply, his hot tongue sweeping into my mouth, making me ache for him. As we kissed, his hands circled my wrists, holding them down onto the mattress gently but firmly. It felt so good, his weight on top of me, holding me in place as his cock slowly worked its way into position.

"Would you like to cum on Daddy's cock, little one?" he asked sweetly, pressing himself against my entrance. I was thrilled. He had seemed to have read my mind.

"Yes, please. I love cumming on your cock, Daddy. It's my favorite," I said, smiling at him.

"I know it is darling. You can cum whenever you like, ok pumpkin?" He questioned.

"Oh, thank you. I need to cum so bad, Daddy," I gushed in relief. I crooned with happiness as he began to sink his cock into me, still holding me by the wrists. He entered me slowly, painfully slow actually. I tried to thrust my hips upwards to take more of him in, but his weight on top of me kept me pinned in place. I whimpered and pouted, but it was to no avail. The pleasure torture wasn't over yet, apparently. He maintained that excruciatingly slow pace until he was buried inside of me completely. He held himself there for a moment before pulling out again at that same incredibly slow speed.

"Daddy," I whined, trying to kick my legs under his heavy weight, trying to shift my hips, anything to stimulate myself.

"Please, I need to cum!" I begged.

"Go ahead, sweet girl," he said, his voice heavy with fake innocence.

"Daddy already told you you could," he said.

"But I need - I need-," I stutter. He was sinking back into me, slowly splitting my pussy open, filling me up inch by inch.

"Please!" I beg.

"What is it that you need sweetheart? You can tell me. You can tell me anything," he said. I could tell he was trying not to smile.

"I need you to fuck me!" I cried out, hardly able to take any more. I needed relief, damn it!

"I am fucking you, sweetheart," he calmly replied. More feigned ignorance. *Cruel bastard.* I was on the verge of tears. His slow pumping felt so good but I just couldn't -

"Please, Daddy," I said, thrashing my head back and forth on the pillow. I was beyond all pride and all embarrassment. I was just pure, throbbing need.

"I need more. Please fuck me hard. I need you to pound me with your cock. Give it to me! Give me your cock, please!" I screamed. He laughed and let go of my wrists at last. I immediately began clawing at his back. I was desperate for release. I would do anything, say anything.

"Anything you say, sweetheart," he said with a sadistic grin and unleashed himself onto me. With wild, animalistic thrusts, he finally gave me the fucking that I needed, that I had begged him for. He spread my legs wide, pounding into me hard and fast. Every thrust made me go blind with pleasure. My whole world was centered on his cock, on the sweet, sweet fucking that he was giving me. I did not last long. I came undone beneath him, trembling as the peak took me over. I grabbed his hips and held on as he growled and pumped as I clenched around him. He pressed his forehead against mine as I relaxed against the sheets once more but did not let up his pace.

"Oh, yes, baby girl. That's so good," he

moaned. His breath grew faster, panting, and growling in her ear. I was still feeling waves of pleasure from orgasm, and with every wild thrust, I could feel myself building towards another. I loved knowing that I was causing so much pleasure in him, knowing that I was making him lose control. His hands grabbed at my breast, squeezing and playing with my nipples just as I had done earlier. We were both covered in sweat, and I could feel his muscles begin to tense, knew that he was getting closer to his climax as well. I could feel my pleasure rise to meet his.

"Oh, fuck, baby. You're so tight, so sexy. You make me so crazy. I'm so close. I love fucking you. I love you," he groaned. His words made me tighten around him, and he drove himself deep inside of me with one last thrust, flooding my pussy with his hot cum. I exploded around him, waves of pure joy and ecstasy overtook me. We shouted as we came together and fell back in a panting, sweaty heap. As I started to get my breath back, it slowly dawned on me what he had said at the very end.

"You love me?" I asked in the darkness. I wished I could see his face better at that moment, but it was still so early that it was dark out and all I could see was his silhouette. He sighed.

"Yes," he admittedly softly.

"I do love you. I've never been as happy as I've been since you came into my life. You're all I've been able to think about. I never knew what it would be like to have someone to come home to, someone to protect and look after. You make me so happy, Molly. You don't have to say it back if it's too early -" He said.

"I love you too," I interrupted, stopping that silly train of thought before it could even leave the station.

"Of course, I love you. You took me in when no one else would have me. You took care of me and made sure that I was happy and healthy. You're sexy and sweet and damn good in bed. How could I help but fall in love with you?" I said.

"Oh, baby girl," he whispered and pulled me close. He kissed me softly on my lips and squeezed me.

"You're more than I ever could have dreamed of. I promise to always be there for you," he said. He held me and kissed me until his alarm clock went off and only then did he reluctantly got out of bed. I studied his well-muscled form as he got dressed, his brown hair shining gold in the early morning light. His toned legs slid into his boxer briefs, and I could still see the swell of his manhood. The sight of him stirred my heart just as much as it did my body.

How did I get so incredibly lucky? I can't believe that he's mine. All mine, I thought, not for the first time and certainly not for the last.

"What would you like for breakfast, baby girl?" he asked, reaching for his pants.

Chapter 19

I never did find an apartment or even look for one, for that matter. A year later, Bill and I are still happily living together. We have settled into a nice routine. Every morning, he updates my itinerary so that I always know where I have to be and when. Then, he makes us breakfast, and we eat in silence. I like it quiet in the mornings. Bill likes it when I give him a blowjob under the table before he leaves for work every morning. He says it is the best part of waking up. If I am home when he returns from work in the evening, he has me meet him by the front door, naked and ready to blow him again. Most nights, the blowing turns to fucking. Sometimes, I am out at a class or my therapy appointment, and he beats me home. On those nights, I get even more vigorous fucking as soon as I walk in the door. Even after a year together, he still can't keep his hands off of me.

As he fucks me, he tells me how much he has missed me and how he couldn't stop thinking about me the whole time we were apart. Often, my itinerary includes taking sexy pics, either in lingerie, he had bought for me or completely naked, and then texting them to him throughout the day. On those days, we fuck all night long.

I still wear my diaper, but not all the time. How little I feel varies from day to day. Both Bill and Dr. Saperstein say that is normal. I still haven't met any other littles, but I would like to. Bill says there are all kinds of littles out there of different genders, ages, and sizes. I'd like to have them all over for a play date someday. I've made a few friends online but no one close by yet. Bill says we will keep looking. I have made other friends, of course. I don't share this particular part of my life with them.

Sometimes, when I am in my little space, I will sleep in my room at night. Having my own space no longer makes me nervous. The first night that I spent in my bed, Daddy gallantly offered to sleep on the floor so that he could catch any monsters that might have been hanging around, looking for little girls to munch on. Knowing that he was nearby and that I was safe made it easy for me to drift off and it hasn't been a problem since. Most nights, however, I sleep in Daddy's bed. He is always coming up with fun, sexy games for us to try and fun, sexy toys for us to play with. I don't always like the games or toys, and he never forces them on me. He is happy to toss them out no matter how much money or time he had spent on them.

"If you're not interested, then neither am I," he would always say and that would be that.

Tonight, we played my favorite game of all. Bill's face wrinkled in concentration. He held his breath, his whole body tense, before letting it out in a triumphant cry.

"Triple word score! Beat that," he yelled and gleefully counted up his points from the Scrabble tiles and added them to the score sheet. I groaned, looking at the numbers in despair. I was whooped.

"Come on, it's your turn," he said, nudging me.

"I don't want to play anymore," I pout.

"What a sore loser!" He exclaimed. I can tell how much he was enjoying this rare opportunity to gloat. I usually had the high score on Scrabble night.

"It's a tactful retreat," I said, trying to sound serious. He starts to tickle me.

"Turn that frown upside down baby girl," he said, making me laugh. Despite my grumpiness over his victory, I giggled. Seeing a crack in my pouting facade, he leaned in for a kiss. As his warm lips covered mine, I immediately forget all about the game. I grabbed onto him like a baby koala, my legs wrapping around his waist and my arms wrapping around his neck. He moans into my mouth, and I can feel him get instantly hard. As our tongues meet, a burning heat stirs inside of me. I am hungry for him. He grabs my ass, leaning me back on the couch and pulling me closer against him. I spread my legs wider, knocking over the board. Tiles are scattered everywhere, but we hardly notice as we tear at each other's clothing. He pulls my shirt off and captures my nipple with his teeth. Knowing just how much pressure to apply, which is a lot, he teases me, watching me writhe beneath him. He squeezes my breasts together and buries his face there, licking and nibbling. I ache to feel his skin on mine and pull at his shirt, whining with impatience as it gets tangled up in his arms.

"Hold on, baby girl," he said, pulling it off for me, "so impatient." He settles back on top of me, and I run my hands over the muscles of his back, over the light sprinkling of hair on his chest, lightly grazing his nipples. Our naked flesh presses together as he kisses me again. He pulls me against him tightly, wrapping me up in his warm, strong arms. I know that I am exactly where I belong. I have finally found my home, and it is here in his arms. He lifts my skirt and takes in a sharp breath of air when he sees that I'm not wearing any panties. I like to surprise him with that every once in a while, and it always gets a reaction. He looks at me like the big bad wolf about to gobble up little red, and the analogy makes me giggle.

"Oh, you're in trouble now, little one," he said with a grin and lowered himself. He takes me in with a deep breath, savoring the scent of me. He teases me lightly with his tongue, grazing my labia and clit casually, not wanting to overwhelm me with too much pleasure at once.

"Hold your legs open for Daddy," he said. I obey, always more than happy to be ordered around by him. His dominance in the bedroom remains one of my favorite things about him. I grip my thighs, holding my legs akimbo as he continues to explore my dripping slit with his tongue. He moans as he tastes me, bathing me with long slow licks. I watch him, hypnotized and he works his way inward, seeking out my clit. I moan when he finds it, almost forgetting to do as he instructed and running my hands through his soft locks instead. Almost. I'm much better trained these days, and I know that will earn me a time-out at the very least.

My hands stay in place as he twirls his tongue around my button. I whimper, my legs quivering as he laps at me faster. He sinks a finger into my tight, hole, looking up at me with an evil glimmer in his eye, knowing that I'm already close to a climax. Only I can't because he hasn't permitted me yet. I know from the look in his eyes that it will be a long evening and that permission is still a long way away. Slowly, he slides in a second finger, stretching me out in the most delicious way. I lose track of everything else in the world; all I am aware of are his fingers pumping in and out of me as his tongue traces circles of ecstasy over my clit. All I can do is hold my legs open and try not to cum like a good girl. Finally, he stops torturing my pussy with pleasure. Standing over me, he pulls his pants and boxers down, freeing his rock hard penis. I can't take my eyes off of it or him as he slowly licks the fingers that have just been inside of me and then wraps them around the head of his cock. He strokes it as he gazes into my eyes, watching my expression get hungrier by the minute. He loves teasing me, making me wait for it, making me beg for it even. He loves to hear me beg.

"Turn over," he said. I shift my weight and roll over onto my tummy.

"Ass in the air," he said. I love this position. His voice is gruff and commanding, making my body thrill with arousal. I am his to command, and he knows it. Again, he makes me wait, ass up, as he pleasures himself. My pussy is throbbing, but I wait, knowing full well that it will be well worth it. He smacks my ass, lightly. This is a sexy spanking, not a punishment spanking. I smile as he spanks me again, just hard enough to sting. Just hard enough to make my pussy tingle. I moan and hold my ass up higher, eager for more spankings. They rain down until my entire ass is on fire and my pussy is dripping onto the couch. I wait, panting in the silence. He grabs me by the hair and brings my mouth to his cock. I lick him eagerly

"That's it, baby," he moaned.

"Suck me down. Take me deep. Daddy's filthy girl," he said as I moan around his cock. I love the dirty names he calls me. I love being dirty for him and him alone. He plunges in cock in deep, making me choke and drool, knowing just how much I can take and just how much will leave me aching for more. He knows that with every thrust down my throat, the fire in my pussy only grows hotter. I make sure to keep my ass in the air, aware that he has not instructed otherwise and that is likely enjoying the view as he slowly fucks my throat.

He sits on the couch and pulls me onto his lap. He pulls my skirt up over my head, leaving me naked. I straddle his lap, and he starts licking and nibbling my breasts again. He positions his cock near my entrance but doesn't plunge in just yet.

"Play with yourself," he muttered around a mouthful of my nipple.

"Let's see how horny baby girl can get," he said, smiling. I rub my clit, driven wild by his mouth on me and by his cock, so tantalizingly close. I know I shouldn't rub too hard, he still hasn't given me permission to cum, but he feels so damn good. He grabs my ass, pulling my cheeks apart, giving them the occasional slap. I know that can tell that I am getting dangerously close.

"Watch it little one. Who do you belong to?" He asked. I whimper softly, but I slow down.

"I belong to you, Daddy," I reply, knowing where this is going.

"And who does this pussy belong to?" He pushes his cock against me, nudging toward my slick entrance. I gasp and moan, trying to find the words he wants to hear.

"This pussy belongs to you," I manage to say between clenched teeth. He sinks into me a little bit deeper, stretching me. His fingers dig into the flesh of my buttocks, tightly controlling the pace, delighting in the way my eyes roll back into my head as he impales me with his cock.

"Good girl," he whispers.

"Nice and slow. That's a good little slut," he said, slapping my ass and groping it with both hands. My back arches as he finally fully inside of me, still playing with my clit.

"Ride me, baby girl," he said, leaning back to enjoy the show. He knows that letting me set the pace is dangerous, that I am liable to forget myself and let myself go before I'm allowed to. I will have to be extra careful. I move my hips slowly, sliding up and down the length of him as I stare into his eyes. I edge myself on his cock, pausing when I need to, gritting my teeth as I use every ounce of my willpower to keep myself from losing control.

"Mmm, my baby girl needs it badly, doesn't she?" He questions.

"Yes, Daddy! I need to cum so bad. Please, please, please ..." I trailed off, so enraptured by lust that I forget to beg. He laughs and twists my nipples lightly, making me gasp.

"Oh, I know you can do better than that. Beg like a good girl and Daddy will let you cum," he said. I whimper and slow down my pace, trying to focus. His cock was so distracting.

"Please, Daddy. I want to cum on your cock so bad. I've been a good girl. Please let me cum. Your cock feels so good, so hard inside my slutty little pussy. Please, Daddy, can I?" I beg.

"Much better," he growls. He grips me by the hips and flips me onto my back, spreading my legs wide as he plunges into me, hard and deep.

"You can cum now, baby girl," he orders. He slams into me, fast and furious. I wrap my thighs around him and hold on as my orgasm erupts. My head snaps back, and I moan with abandon. He has turned me into quite the screamer.

"That's right, sweetie, cum for Daddy," he said. He kisses my sweaty neck, and I tremble underneath him. Shivers of pleasure run through me even after the main wave breaks. His thrusts do not slow down, he keeps pounding into me, wrapped up in his own pleasure now.

"Oh, darling. You get so wet when you cum —

such a sweet, dirty girl. You make Daddy feel so good," he said. I love how vocal he gets when he fucks me. I never get tired of being reassured that I am his fantasy, his perfect girl. His hands clench and unclench, and I know that he is close.

"Fuck yeah, baby girl. Keep taking it just like that. Oh, you're such a good girl. Daddy's good little slut. Here it comes!" He moans. He goes completely still, except for his cock which is pumping away inside of me, filling me with hot cum. With a groan, he goes limp against me, burying his head into my breast. He holds me close to him, still inside me, until he regains his breath. A feeling of complete contentment washes over me. I know that in a moment, we will have to clean up the substantial mess we've made but for now, I hold his sweaty brow to my chest and thank my lucky stars that he came into my life.

Chapter 20

That evening, as he is giving me my bath, he starts asking me about vacation spots. At first, it seems like another fun game, fantasizing about all the exotic places we would like to travel to someday. As the discussion gets more and more specific, with details about vacation time and airfare, I realize that it's more than that.

"Wait, are you serious?" I ask. I have never been on a trip before, and the idea is exciting.

"Well, maybe not right away. I was just sort of thinking, you know …" He trailed off and blushed. I hadn't seen him blush since he asked me to move in with him.

"You were thinking …" I prompted. What on earth could have him so nervous?

"I was thinking, well I was wondering, actually, where you might want to go when we went on our honeymoon … someday … maybe…" He blushed, even more, deeper than I had ever seen before.

"Did you - did you just propose to me?" I questioned. A surge of adrenaline swept over my body.

"No!" he sputtered.

"I wouldn't propose to you in a bathroom. I would do it nicer than that. You know, romantic. Rinse," he said. I leaned my head back as he rinsed the suds from my hair. Silently, I think about what he said as he helps me out of the bathtub and dries my hair. He towels me off and helps me into my pajamas, tonight I've chosen a diaper and a onesie. He combs my hair and splits my hair into pigtails, fastening them with small rubber bands. He carries me to bed and finds Hamilton, putting him on the pillow beside me.

"Tahiti," I say, finally reaching a decision.

"What?" he asks, seemingly forgotten the topic at hand.

"For our honeymoon. I think I would like to go to Tahiti. I hear it's beautiful. What do you think?" I ask, smiling. He grinned, leaning down to kiss my forehead.

"I think I'd better start planning a trip to Tahiti," he said winking at me.

Who is Tina Moore?

Tina Moore has enjoyed the lifestyle of a Mommy Domme for several years. She began exploring kink and BDSM in her youth and found her love of being a strict Mommy Domme in early 2000. Tina Moore is now an author of many MDLG, DDLG and ABDL themed novels.

Follow her on:

Author Page on Amazon

Instagram @tinamoore.kdp

If you enjoyed this book, it would be much appreciated if you leave **a review on Amazon**.

www.ingramcontent.com/pod-product-compliance
Lightning Source LLC
Chambersburg PA
CBHW031017190726
48286CB00003BA/894